Winter of the Wolf
Terry Hebert

Copyright © 2019 Terry Hebert
All rights reserved. No part of this book may be reproduced or transmitted in any form or by any means, electronic or mechanical, including photocopying, recording or by any information storage and retrieval system, without permission in writing from the publisher.

Any resemblance to persons living or dead, as well as any location, event, or entity is purely coincidental. This novel is a work of fiction.

Yellow Rose Publications—Miami, FL
ISBN: 978-0-578-54625-4
Winter of the Wolf
Terry Hebert
Available Formats: eBook | Paperback distribution

Dedication

This book is dedicated to my family who encouraged me and refused to let me give up on my dream to become an author - no matter how many times I doubted myself.

Chapter One
December 6th
11:55 PM

The wolf pack moved quickly and silently through the small fishing/hunting camp located high in the mountains of Colorado. Consisting of three males and three females, this was a larger group than most, but they had been together long enough to hunt efficiently together. Unfortunately, with winter weather beginning to move in, game was getting harder for the pack to find, especially for a pack of this size. They had been forced to move further and deeper South over the last three months into terrain they had never hunted in before. In the 1940's the population of gray wolves had gotten so large and caused so much damage to the area ranchers that the state of Colorado had allowed hunters to come in to hunt them. A bounty was paid for every wolf that was turned into authorities. The result was that the majority of the population had been decimated and those wolves that weren't killed had moved into Montana and Wyoming to escape execution.

The sudden exodus allowed the over-population problem to resolve itself. However, in the last few years, the grays had been re-introduced back into Colorado in small packs, like this one. Today, the state no longer allows the slaughter of the wolves for profit, so the packs have been able to once again make their home in the Colorado wilderness.

Tonight a bright full moon was hanging high in the sky as they moved stealthily through the surrounding forest growth and there was a bite to the wind. The pack knew instinctively that winter would soon be upon them. This made their search for food all the more desperate. It had been a week since their last good feeding when the pack had been able to take down a doe. Now, fighting against their natural instincts to avoid humans at all cost, they were forced to come into the secluded Rocky Mountain hunting/fishing camp hoping to find something they could scavenge. Being careful to stay hidden within the thick, dark shadows that clung to the small log shelters, the pack began to search the alleys and ditches for anything edible.

Following their highly sensitive noses, the wolves scented the air and instantly became excited by the amount of discarded food they detected laying within the tall metal cans standing like sentinels behind each of the log cabins. The scent of humans hung heavy in the air, but in their excitement and urgent need to feed, the younger wolves became careless and knocked over two of the cans. The sudden loud crash that resulted startled them momentarily, but the smell of rotting food was simply too enticing to resist and they all quickly went back to scrounging through the discarded cans and wrappers.

The raucous noise disrupted the silent night and alerted the slumbering hunting dog currently staying in cabin number four to the intruder s. Jumping to his feet, he immediately began barking a warning.

"Shut up, you damn stupid dog," Big Mike Townsend told his four-year old hound, Heck. "You're making so much noise, I can't play my cards!"

"Hell, Mike, you can't play cards when it's quiet!" Pete joked good-naturedly.

"Yeah, you can't blame the dog for THAT!" laughed Buddy. "You just naturally suck at it!"

Suitably embarrassed, Big Mike took a swig of his luke-warm beer and replied, "Awe, shut up and get ready to pay up." Laying down his cards, he added, "I've got three kings, assholes. What have you got?"

Still, the dog continued to bark aggressively at the closed door.

"I've got a queen high heart flush. Guess this pot is mine!" offered Pete.

Laying his cards on the table with a flourish, Buddy said, "Sorry, gents. Full house - tens over sevens," and raked in the pot money.

"Damn it! That's it," Big Mike yelled. Throwing down his cards and stomping over to the door, he opened it and Heck went charging out into the night. "Get outta here!"

Rubbing his hands together, the man turned around wide a wide grin and said, "Now maybe we can get down to playing some real cards, eh, guys?" causing all three to laugh out loud.

The trio had first met at the camp six years earlier, and became instant friends. Since then they returned at the same time every year to catch up. Though none of them actually did any hunting while they were there, they used this time together drinking heavily, playing cards and generally just enjoying the break from their otherwise mundane lives.

Pete Erenburg was the youngest of the three and had worked as an accountant for his father at a small shipping company in Atlanta for the past twelve years. He was your stereo-typical nerd complete with black horn-rimmed glasses and a clear plastic pocket protector. Married for 25 years to his high school sweetheart, Bess, he was the consummate family man. Pete also had two children who were currently both away at college. Their combined tuition made money extremely tight, but these trips were his only guilty pleasure, and he made a point to never miss one. Truth be told, Bess looked forward to them as much as he did.

Wes "Buddy" Willowby was just a good old boy from Murfreesboro, Arkansas where he had worked for the U.S. Army Corps of Engineers since he got out of the army in 1991 and was currently responsible for maintaining the Narrows Dam located on the Missouri River. When he had first applied, he hadn't planned on it becoming a long-term career choice, but he found out quickly that he truly enjoyed the work and loved living in the Ozarks. The fresh air and smell of the pines was intoxicating. Although he had never owned a gun in his life, he was an avid fisherman and spent as much of his free time as possible on nearby Lake Greeson pulling in big mouth bass and flathead catfish. With no wife or children to be concerned with, he considered these annual forays into the Rocky Mountains a gift he gave to himself.

The third member of the group was Mike Townsend. True to his nickname, "Big Mike" was a definite force to be reckoned with. At a height of 6 feet 11 inches and weighing close to 450 pounds, he cast a huge shadow wherever he went. In college, he had been able to keep lean and fit as a starting full back for the Aggies at Texas A & M in College Station and he had always planned to go into the pros after graduation. Unfortunately, those dreams were crushed when after barely graduating with a degree in animal husbandry; his father had insisted that he return home to work on the family's dairy farm. The farm had been in his family for four generations, and he was destined to inherit it after his father's death three years later. Bored with the life he was irrevocably chained to, he struggled to keep the dairy in the black, but the stress and expense of running such an operation soon caused him to develop a taste for alcohol, fried foods and fast women, all of which had contributed to his present condition. After four marriages (and four divorces), he had turned to food and drink as a way to find comfort. He knew his college classmates would not recognize the man he was today, and he couldn't care less. His friends from school had written him off years ago. Pete, Buddy and

Heck were the only friends he had in his life now, and he was fine with that, too.

Outside, Heck continued to raise a ruckus, only now the barking had a frenzied madness to it that Big Mike had never heard come out of the hound before. With a frown creasing his wide forehead, he stopped halfway back to the table and turned back toward the door. He recognized the sounds of a vicious dog fight begin outside. Big Mike knew that Heck could handle himself in any conflict, but this didn't sound like a single dog. No, it definitely sounded as if his dog was being attacked. He moved quickly over to the door of the cabin. The other two men got up and headed for the door as well, more curious than concerned until they heard Heck's distinctive baying bark become a short sharp yelp, and then nothing at all. The sudden silence was somehow worse than the previous cacophony of noise had been. Opening the door, the three men walked out into the cold night, but failed to see the dog anywhere.

With a sharp whistle, Big Mike shouted, "Here, Heck. Come on, boy". Normally, Heck would have come running full blast from wherever he was in answer to his master's voice, but this time Big Mike got no response.

Perplexed by his dog's disappearance, Big Mike moved off the front porch and onto the gravel drive. Hearing snorting and slurping sounds from the side of the cabin, the men walked cautiously to peer around the corner. The sight before them was something out of a nightmare. The wolf pack had literally torn the dog to pieces and was eating ravenously from the bloody viscera. Gristle and gore covered their fur causing them to look like mythical Hell hounds. Pete immediately turned and threw up against the side of the building while Buddy turned and ran back inside the cabin slamming the door behind him.

Seeing the carnage in front of him and recognizing the victim of the wolf attack as Heck, Big Mike was immediately filled with rage and without giving any thought to what he was about to do, he rushed into the gory scene. Slipping on the bloody mess of the dog's entrails, he fell hitting his head on the blacktop hard enough to see stars. Stunned, he sat up and shook his head to clear away the cobwebs. Opening his eyes, he found himself looking directly into the vivid blue eyes of a massive white and grey wolf standing less than three feet away from him. Obviously the leader of the pack, the alpha was focused on the obese man growling threateningly and showing his long, sharp teeth stained with meat and sinew from Heck. Big Mike was more scared in that moment than he had ever been in his life and he felt his bladder let loose. As he began to slowly crab crawl backwards in the direction of the cabin, he never took his eyes off the formidable beast before him. The wolf continued to watch his retreat silently. When he was about six feet away from the gruesome spectacle, Big Mike turned around and got to his knees. With tears running down his cheeks, he started to rise with the intent of returning to the cabin as quickly as possible just as his two companions had done. Suddenly, he felt an acute pain in his right calf that caused him to cry out. Looking back at his leg, he was horrified to find that the alpha wolf had sunk those dangerously sharp teeth deeply into the meaty flesh and easily slicing through the fabric of big man's jeans and thermal underwear. The ice blue eyes remained focused on the man while blood ran freely between the imbedded teeth. Screaming desperately for help from his now absent friends, Big Mike kicked back with his left foot as hard as he could. The steel-toed boot connected squarely with the wolf's nose causing the canine to yelp in pain and instantly release its hold on his leg. While the alpha was whining and frantically rubbing at his nose in the dirt, the man took advantage of the opportunity and instantly rose up onto his feet. Favoring his bloodied right leg, Big Mike limped back into the safety of the log cabin.

Once the big gray had recovered from the brutal kick from the man's boot it was no longer interested in the corpse of the dog. He trotted off down the street, the other members of the pack immediately following behind. Other dogs inside the small cabins around the camp continued to bark out their warnings as the wolves returned quickly and silently back into the shadowy shelter of the forest.

Chapter Two

January 14th
Dallas, Texas

She had heard the phrase "You can never go home again" all of her life, but she had never thought it would actually apply to her. When Becca Thornton left Colorado for Texas fourteen years earlier, she truly believed she would never go back again. As a child, she had despised the winters and the boredom they inevitably brought with them. As a result, she couldn't wait until she graduated high school and could drive south watching the Rocky Mountains disappear from her rear view mirror. While still a senior, Becca had applied to numerous colleges from California to Florida, but nothing north of the Mason/Dixon line. She didn't care if she ever saw snow again, and with a 4.0 average and glowing recommendations from both her teachers and a few prominent members of the community, it wasn't long before the acceptance letters began arriving. The decision to go to school out of state might not have been what her parents had wanted for her, but she was determined to go. Eli and Marie doted on their only child, denying her nothing throughout her childhood, so they had reluctantly agreed to her wishes.

After reviewing the multitude of offers she received, Becca ultimately decided to accept the one she had received from Southern Methodist University in Dallas. This was partly due to the lucrative scholarship program they promised, partly because of the outstanding legal studies the Dedman School of Law offered, and partly because snow was practically non-existent this far South in Texas. So, the week after graduation, she began preparing for her new life.

Becca's family had owned Silver Dollar Ranch for five generations. That wasn't the original name, of course, but Becca's Great Grandfather re-named it not for the silver coins that the name would imply, but by the bounty of Quaking Aspen trees that he always called Silver Dollars because of the way the leaves shimmered in the wind. The ranch was one of the largest working cattle ranches and quarter horse farms in the state of Colorado. When her grandfather had died in 1989, her mother had inherited the ranch and all of its holdings, which were extensive.

Wanting to capitalize on its well-regarded reputation, her parents came up with the idea to create a way for city dwellers to actively participate in ranch life. To this end, they took a few acres and built twenty self-contained cabins along the creek that ran through the property. Interested visitors looking to capture a bit of the old west could take part in the cattle round-ups, feeding the stock and go on supervised trail rides. Overnight camp-outs and the fishing and hunting forays her father lead into the mountains soon became a favorite activity for many vacationers. Once word began to spread, the reservations began pouring in and the Silver Dollar Dude Ranch was able to pay off their massive construction loan in less than two years. While Becca's parents made sure that she never wanted for anything, she still wasn't happy and it wasn't just with the weather. With the addition of the dude ranch, her summers became completely occupied with working around the place. Her parents paid her a small salary, but with entertaining the paying customers, cleaning the cabins, helping her father guide the overnight trips, and the other myriad of chores found around a working guest ranch, she found that she had very little time for herself. Oh, how she longed for the day she could make her great escape.

When that day finally came and she arrived on the SMU campus the fall of 1999, Becca felt a euphoric sense of relief for several reasons. August in Texas carries with it temperatures in excess of 100 degrees, and she literally basked in the heat. Also, she wasn't the spoiled rich kid anymore. At a school where most of the students were privileged and came from well-to-do families, she was just one of the crowd and very grateful for the lack of notoriety. She devoted most of her time to her studies, which were challenging to say the least, but also enjoyed volunteering part-time in the school's library. This got her out of the noisy dorm and allowed her plenty of quiet solitude to study her law books.

At the end of her freshman year, her father was killed suddenly in a freak accident while on a fishing trip into the mountains with some of his paying guests. His horse had stumbled over a particularly rocky part of the trail, slipped, and both rider and horse went off the side into a deep ravine. Even then her father might have survived, except that the horse and all the gear had landed on top of him instantly crushing the life out of him. Becca flew home for the burial, but returned to Dallas the very next day, leaving her disappointed mother and the ranch foreman to handle the massive amount of work required.

In 2004, Becca graduated with a law degree in the top 5% of her class and was fiercely pursued by several prestigious law firms in Dallas, Baton Rouge, Tallahassee, and Houston. Her mother had apologized for not attending the graduation ceremonies, but responsibilities at the ranch had made that impossible. Becca understood. After all, her own goals and commitments had kept her from going home for years. At least that's what she told herself, and when she accepted the position as an attorney for Booker, Hutchins, Thompson and Haynes specializing in fraud cases, she had moved on and never looked back. Within a year, her work ethic and doggedness toward details had her on the fast track for junior partner.

What she didn't know at the time was that her mother hadn't come to her graduation not so much because of the distance, but due to her declining health. She simply hadn't wanted to worry Becca. Then in 2009, after months of suffering severe headaches and dizziness that she consistently blamed on her age, increasing speech problems, a trouble performing simple tasks and sudden shifts in her behavior where she would lash out at the workers over the most minor things, Marie was suddenly stricken with a seizure that left her unconscious and unresponsive. Floyd Furlong, the ranch foreman, had found her on the floor of the horse barn and immediately called 911. Becca was notified by Marie's doctor that a tumor the size of a large egg had been found in her brain and she was going to need surgery right away to have any hope of recovery. Becca immediately took a leave of absence and flew to Denver so she could be with her mother during and after her surgery. The doctor was pleased to let Becca know that the surgery had gone splendidly and assured her that he had removed all of the tumor, but added that her mother would never be the same as she was before and that she would need to have constant care for the rest of her life to ensure that another tumor didn't form. Becca was stunned, but after notifying her boss of the circumstances, she began searching for an assisted care facility in the Dallas area that could accommodate her mother. In May of that same year, Becca moved her mother to Dallas and her new home leaving Floyd and his wife, Frieda, to continue running the ranch in her absence.

Becca's life continued moving in the systematic way she had arranged it, except that now there was one more piece added to the puzzle. Every Sunday, Becca would spend the day with her mother at the care facility reading to her, feeding her meals, and talking about things going on in the world. Most of the time these things were met with silence and blank stares as her mother's memory and focus declined, but every so often, a light of recognition would shine from Marie's pale blue eyes and for at least a little while, Becca had her mother back. This is the way it went until last week when Becca got the inevitable call from the director of the nursing home to tell her that Marie was gone. She had apparently died peacefully during the night after the nurse checked on her around midnight and was found at 7AM the next morning by her caretaker. In her hand she clutched a picture of Becca sitting astride Angel, the Palomino pony she had loved as a teenager.

Becca contacted Floyd to let him know the circumstances, who in turn, contacted the family's attorney in Lake City. Roger Whitmire had been a long-time friend of Eli and Marie Thornton and had handled all of their legal matters for as long as Becca could remember, so it was no surprise to her when he called her regarding her mother's passing.

"Good afternoon, Rebecca. This is Roger Whitmire, your mother's attorney." It was never just Becca with him and she wondered again why he felt it necessary to always explain who he was whenever they spoke even though the man had practically been a member of her family for the majority of her life.

"Yes, Roger. I thought I would be hearing from you soon. As my mother's executrix, I wanted to find out what arrangements have been made, if any," Becca asked.

"Your mother was very explicit about that. Understandably, she wants to be buried in the glen on the ranch next to your father. I have already notified Abernathy's Funeral Home to expect her body to be coming from Dallas as soon as it can be arranged. I've also gone ahead and spoken to Father Bingham about the service. He wanted me to assure you that he is available to hold the service at your convenience. You should know that although your mother's passing was sudden and unexpected, as you are the only child and there are no liens against the estate, you will naturally inherit everything - the ranch, all of the livestock, cash and an assortment of stocks, bonds and investments all of which add up to a considerable monetary total." After a moment of silence and a clearing of his throat, Lawyer Whitmire continued.

"However, what you may not be aware of is that after your father's death when you chose to take up permanent residence in Texas, Marie added a codicil to her will. In it, she stated that upon her death you would take over the day-to-day operations of the ranch and all businesses and responsibilities relating to it."

"What are you talking about?" Becca exclaimed, surprised by the news. "Mother knew I had established my law career here and that I loved living in Texas. We had talked about it several times."

"Be that as it may, the codicil goes on to say that should you refuse this duty, the ranch and its holdings, along with all monies, would be liquidated and the revenue donated to the National Park Service save for a small annual stipend of $75,000 per year to be paid to Floyd and Frieda Newman for their many years of faithful service to the family." Here he stopped for a moment before adding, "In short, Rebecca, your mother made it so that if you do not return to take charge of the Silver Dollar Ranch in residence, you will receive nothing from your her estate."

Chapter Three

January 16th
Southeast Colorado

He lay on the flat stone watching the rest of the pack feed. It had been a small meal, but the first he had been able to provide for them in the last few days. It wasn't enough by any means, but it was at least something in their empty stomachs. When his mate had finished eating, she came over to join him on the rock, licking the remaining blood from the rabbit off her fur. The alpha male enjoyed having her warmth near him to help combat the freezing cold, but he remained alert, his ice blue eyes constantly scanning the shadows for trouble or potential prey. The recent episode at the silver mine had made him tense and more than a little wary.

Nearly three weeks ago, the pack had been comfortably living in a small, but dry den about 35 miles away and it had been easy to catch their fill in food. Then one morning they had been roused by the acrid smell of diesel fuel and the noise of machines and the loud voices of men. Game soon became almost impossible to find, because of the noise the men made working both day and night had scared them off. So the wolves had begun venturing into the work camp under the cover of darkness to scavenge through the discarded trash for their meals. Usually they were able to find plenty of discarded food to satisfy their hunger, and none of the men seemed to notice or care. It seemed to be the perfect symbiotic relationship. Until one night while they were feeding, one of the men came to drop a bag of trash in the landfill and saw the wolves digging through the refuse. Though the wolves only watched him warily and never made any aggressive moves toward him, the man had dropped the bag spilling it greasy contests and gone screaming back to the shelter of the cabins where he raised the alarm that wolves were inside the camp. The pack took off immediately for the shelter of their den.

The next night at dusk, there was a man waiting at the dump when the wolves came out of the woods to feed. Using a rifle with a night scope, he took careful aim on one of the females and put a single bullet directly into her head. The rest of the wolves were so startled by the unexpected sound of the gun, they immediately took to the shelter of the woods. Even though the dead bitch was an elder in the pack, she was still a breeder and in a pack this small, breeding females were important to the continuing growth of the group. The remaining members whimpered in fear and comforted each other throughout the night.

When darkness fell again, the wolves had returned to the landfill for food, only to once again have the hunter shoot at them. This time, however, the bullet only injured the target by entering the left hindquarter of one of the male wolves, but the alpha male reacted immediately. Snarling and with teeth bared, the massive gray beast charged toward the man much faster than expected, and his jaw clamped down on the man's forearm. His sharp teeth sank deep into the flesh and he began shaking his head viciously from left to right. The hunter shrieked in pain as he was jerked back and forth by the 185 pound male, but the big wolf held the man's arm in its vice-like grip. Immediately the gray's mate charged the man and bit into soft flesh high on the man's thigh. The rest of the pack also struck creating a blur of blood, teeth and fur around the hunter. The man dropped his now useless gun, and desperately tried to free himself from the assault, but to no avail. Blood, tissue, and saliva flew in all directions while the man continued to scream. With a snarl, the Alpha sunk its teeth into the throat of the man, releasing a torrent of blood. From the direction of the mining camp, flashlights and shouting alerted the alpha that more men were coming. Releasing their hold on the dying man, the wolves reluctantly returned back into the woods. Instinct told the big gray that their den would no longer be safe, so he didn't lead them back to it. Instead, he led them farther away and deeper into the dense Rio Grande National forest.

When the sun came up the next morning, the pack had traveled nearly 17 miles from the mine. The taste of the hunter's hot blood had only worked to make them even hungrier than before. Exhausted and nearly starving, the injured male was weak from blood loss and he moved slowly. The leader knew he had to find shelter and food quickly. When he sniffed the air, he could also sense a coming change in the winter weather that would bring ice and snow with it. While he knew the pack could last a few more days without food, finding water and dry shelter for the group was something that couldn't wait. The injured young wolf was painfully dragging his leg now making progress even slower. In addition, though early in the pregnancy, his alpha female was carrying her first litter and would need a place to whelp the pups within the next couple of months.

Two days later, the pack came across an outcropping of boulders near a small running stream. There was a space between the boulders, and by digging out the loose dirt in and around the gap, the wolves were able to enlarge the area to a size that accommodated the entire group. Though not as large as their previous den, it would still offer them warmth and badly needed protection from the approaching storm.

Chapter Four

January 17TH
Dallas, Texas

Becca had requested Attorney Whitmire to fax a copy of her mother's will to her, which he did. She then took it to one of her "girls night out" group who happened to also be an attorney in the Estate Remediation department at the law firm where she worked and asked if she would mind reviewing it to see if there was any way she could beat the codicil her mother had made to the original document. Unfortunately, after a couple of days the attorney let her know that the will was iron clad, and she could find no loophole that would help break it. Having no other option, Becca was forced to give a week's notice to her boss, and leave the life she had worked so hard to build for herself.

So it was that a week after her mother's death, Becca was loading the last of her suitcases into her Jeep Wrangler. The movers had come that morning and loaded all of her furniture and packing boxes into their truck. It hadn't taken them long to load the few pieces she owned and they confirmed with her that they would meet her at the ranch in a few days depending on the weather. Still reeling about the sudden turn of events her life had taken, she had decided that her best plan of action was get up to the ranch and then take some time to decide whether or not to keep it or liquidate everything. It would take her two days to make the trip, so she was packing a small cooler with snacks and bottled water to take along. By the time she had everything ready to go, she found that she was physically exhausted. All she wanted to do was go to bed and get a fresh start in the morning, but that was not to be. Sadie, her 2-year old black lab, was whining at the door to go out.

"Okay, girl, I hear you. Let's go." Pulling her hair up into a rough ponytail and tugging her Dallas Cowboys ball cap down on her head, she grabbed the dog leash from the table. Becca clipped it onto the dog's collar and the duo stepped outside.

January in Texas is typically cold, but not bitterly. However, with the sun going down and shadows lengthening as they began their walk, Becca was glad she had chosen to grab a heavier jacket when she left the apartment.

"Let's make this quick, what do you say?"

Momentarily distracted by her mistress's voice, Sadie looked up expectantly for what she hoped would be a treat, but the moment was cut short when a calico cat darted across their path. Barking sharply, the dog yanked hard on the leash pulling Becca off balance. The unexpected move caused her to let go of the leash and Sadie seized the opportunity to pursue the offending feline.

"Sadie! No!" Becca shouted, but the lab was having too much fun to listen. "Just perfect" she muttered to herself, and she began the chase in earnest. After running a block and a half, she was able to get control again when she found Sadie excitedly investigating an enticing scent on a nearby light pole. "That's enough of that, young lady. You'll have lots to chase once we get to the mountains, so save it. There's not much else to do there, but chase chipmunks anyway," Becca mused as she turned them back towards home.

Once inside her condo, Becca began listening to some music from her I-phone as she prepared a sandwich that would work as her dinner since everything else had been thrown out or given away. Before grabbing a Dr. Pepper out of the fridge, she filled Sadie's dish with kibbles and topped off her water bowl. The dog immediately began eating her kibbles, cleaning out the food bowl before Becca even had a chance to sit down on the window seat with her own meal. Becca stared out of the window at the Dallas skyline while she chewed the peanut butter and jelly sandwich ruminating about whether or not she had taken care of everything that she needed to before heading out in the morning. Her mother's body had already been shipped to Abernathy's Funeral Home in Lake City for preparation and ultimate burial. Once again she thought about the route she would be taking the next day. She planned to stop the first night in Raton, New Mexico fairly early in the afternoon so that she could get a good night's sleep before facing the long and arduous drive through the mountains. The weatherman had warned of a bad storm front that would be moving into the region and the roads could become treacherous, Becca knew from past experience. In fact, if the weather turned extremely hazardous, it wasn't uncommon for the highways through the mountains to be closed until passable.

After cleaning up and taking the remaining trash out to the dumpster, Becca undressed and got into the shower. The hot spray sluiced over her body and she let it pound the stress out of her back and shoulders until all the hot water was used up. It felt as if her legs no longer had enough strength left in them to support her when she finally stepped out of the shower, and wrapped herself in a soft white towel. As usual, Sadie was waiting for her on the bath rug when she emerged and watched her while she wiped the condensation off the mirror. Picking up a comb, she pulled it through her wet dark red hair and then applied a light moisturizer to her skin. Becca paused and took a long contemplative look at herself in the mirror. At 32 years, her green eyes were still large and clear and her skin was flawless. She had no crow's feet to speak of yet, and that was good. The smattering of freckles she'd had since she was a kid in Colorado still covered her nose no matter how she tried to hide them. She'd always enjoyed working out, and her tall, slim body continuously drew lustful looks from the men and envious glances from the ladies at the 24 Hour Fitness exercise club. Shaking her head ruefully, she guessed that she was attractive enough, although she just couldn't see that she was anything special. Whatever the reason, the men she worked with seemed interested enough and she certainly received her share of wolf whistles from the men she passed on the street.

Dating simply wasn't something high on her priority list, but there was never a shortage of willing companions when a plus one was needed. The few men she had gone out with consistently told her how beautiful she was. Becca was never certain of their sincerity, though, and never took their compliments seriously. That was probably why she had never let anyone inside the protective bubble she had purposely created around her. Trust had always been a difficult thing for her to give, and besides, her focus had always been on her career. She knew that the rest would come later, but for now Becca was content with the way things were.

Becca hung the towel over the shower rod to dry and slipped into a pair of her favorite cotton pajamas. Then, with Sadie following closely behind, she moved to stand beside the air mattress lying on her bedroom floor. Looking from the makeshift pallet to Sadie and back again, she teased, "Definitely not the Adolphus, but right now I'm just too tired to care."

Crawling onto the bed and pulling the blanket up to her chin, she was actually surprised at how comfortable the mattress was. Sadie curled up next to her and both were asleep within minutes.

Chapter Five

January 20th
Southeastern Colorado

Mitch Vargas was miserable. Two weeks ago his mother had told him that plans had been made for he and his mother's latest boyfriend to spend some time "getting to know each other better" while camping up in the mountains. Since that announcement, he had done everything he could think of to dissuade her from what was undoubtedly a disaster waiting to happen, even going so far as to cry in front of her, but nothing had worked. It wasn't so much that he didn't want to go. He had always loved the mountains and the memory of camping with his dad while he had still been alive was some of his best memories ever, but it just wasn't the same now. Besides, he absolutely couldn't stand his mother's latest conquest - a body builder named Rico, with muscles as big as boulders and the IQ of an insect. The amount of cheap cologne he wore couldn't mask the overwhelming scent of body odor the rolled off the man in waves. This lack of personal hygiene had led Mitch to secretly rename him Reek-O. Even now, thinking about the nickname made him giggle to himself. It was so bad that he simply couldn't fathom why the smell didn't seem to bother his mother at all! The pair had been seeing each other for nearly four months now, and it was becoming painfully obvious, even to a twelve year old boy, that this one wasn't be going away any time soon.

Since his father had died in Fallujah two years ago when an IAD had destroyed the truck he had been riding on in the convoy he had been leading, his mother had had no shortage of "friends" coming round. Most of them didn't hold her interest for too long, and she sent them away fairly quickly, but Rico was different. Mitch certainly understood why the man stuck around. His mother was more than just beautiful. She was stunning. Statuesque and graceful, the heads of both men and women turned whenever she walked by. He had even overheard some of the guys from his school comment that she was a real M.I.L.F., and although he wasn't sure exactly what the anagram meant, he knew it had something to do with her good looks. Her skin was unblemished and the color of fresh honey. Her eyes were large and the color of melted dark chocolate. Mitch especially loved her long, thick black hair that hung straight down her back and ended just below her waist, but it was obvious even to twelve year old Mitch that what drew men to her like flies to sugar was her body. A perfect 38-22-36, Mitch knew just how hard Roxanne Wolfe worked to keep her body in shape. Every day when he would come through the door after school, his mother would just be waking up and getting ready to go to her job at the night club where she danced. The clean smell of her gardenia scented body lotion filled the room. One of his favorite things to do was to sit and watch her apply her exotic make-up. Sometimes she would let him brush her luxurious hair until it shined like a raven's wing. That was the best. During those times, they would talk about his day at school and all of the things they dreamed about doing together one day, but by unspoken agreement they would never talk about his father. Mitch knew that the memories hurt his mother too much, and he hated to see her cry. Instead, he would talk to his father's picture before he fell asleep each night and tell him about her latest lotharios.

By far, the hardest thing he had to do was watch her leave every evening, because he knew he wouldn't see her again until the morning. He feared that, like his father, she would leave one night and simply not come back to him. Mitch didn't know exactly where his mother worked, but he knew she had to be really good because she always brought home lots of cash. He asked her about it once and she told him that the money came from people who really appreciated her dancing. After she would leave for work, he would fix himself a sandwich and spend the rest of the evening doing his homework or watching television before taking a shower and putting himself to bed around 10:00.

"It won't be like this forever, mi pequeño," she would flash her perfect smile and promise him. "One day I'll find a nice man who will love us and take care of us and I won't have to do this work anymore. Then we'll be able to make up for all of the time we've lost. In the meantime, we only have each other and we're doing alright. Right?"

Then she would wrap her arms around him and smother him with kisses until he begged her to stop. Mitch didn't doubt that one day her dream would come true, but with the kind of losers his mom had been bringing home lately, he hoped it wouldn't be any time soon. Unfortunately, his mom seemed to be as excited as Mitch was miserable with Rico and so he did his best to make her happy by agreeing to go on this stupid camping trip in the Rocky Mountains. Now here he was – cold, miserable, and bored out of his mind. He couldn't wait for this particular nightmare to be over.

Adding another log to the already blazing fire, Rico asked Mitch if he was getting hungry. When he received no answer from the boy, he stopped what he was doing and growled, "Look kid. I didn't want to do this trip any more than you did, but your mom and I have a good thing going on and I don't want to blow it because you have some kind of a problem with me. Roxie wants us to work things out and she thought this might be a good way to do it. She said you liked camping, so here we are. Face it, kid. I'm not going anywhere, so you just need to deal with it."

"Roxanne," Mitch mumbled.

"What? Did you say something to me?"

Looking Rico straight in the eyes, he said clearly, "My mother's name is Roxanne, not Roxie."

With a chuckle and a roll of the eyes, Rico responded, "Whatever, kid. Look, why don't we try doing some hunting before it gets too dark. What do you say?"

Mitch looked at the muscle-man like horns had just sprouted from his forehead. He couldn't be serious, could he? They had brought plenty of food with them, more than they needed for the weekend, so there was no need to kill anything. Part of what Mitch loved most about the mountains was the quiet solitude and undisturbed beauty of the wilderness. He relished the whispering of the trees whenever a breeze came through and the furtive sounds of wildlife moving through the undergrowth. This was something that his father had instilled in him when he was still a little kid. Their camping and fishing trips had been all the more special because they had shared this love of nature. The thought of seeing this peaceful sanctuary disrupted by gunfire where some innocent animal would be killed and skinned made his stomach roll with nausea. He watched as Rico walked into the tent and was shocked to see the man return with a rifle. Mitch's eyes widened at the sight. He hadn't even known that the man had brought a gun!

Checking to make sure there was a round ready in the chamber, Rico looked straight at the boy and said, "Come on, kid. Let's get this show on the road!"

"You're kidding, right?" Mitch asked incredulously. "You can't be serious."

With a smirk, Rico replied, "Hell yeah, I'm serious. So, get your pansy-ass up off that rock and let's get a move on."

When Mitch didn't immediately rise, the big man lost patience with him. Turning blazing eyes on the boy, he shouted angrily, "Now!"

Realizing this nightmare just took a turn for the worse as a frigid light rain began to fall, Mitch stood up and brushed the detritus off the seat of his pants. Reluctantly following several steps behind the man with the gun, the boy trudged along miserably.

Chapter Six

The pack had been forced to move slowly to allow the injured male wolf to keep up, and still he continued to drag his leg, falling further and further behind. Blood continued to run down the side of its body. Although it had slowed some, the smell of the fresh blood only increased the hunger of the remaining members of the pack, but they continued to encourage the male to move along with sharp barks and by gently nudging him when he'd fall too far behind. Struggling against the burning pain, he had to make frequent stops to rest.

The alpha male never slowed down as the wounded wolf grew weaker. He instinctively understood the urgency and that he had to get the pack back to the den and as far away from the men as quickly as possible.

Chapter Seven

Rico had been walking through the cold rain for almost an hour with Mitch following a few yards behind when he suddenly stopped and brought his rifle up. Not watching where he was going, the boy walked right into his back. Surprised by the sudden impact, Rico glared down at the boy and held a finger up to his mouth indicating that he should be quiet as he brought the rifle back into position. Mitch nodded disinterestedly and stepped back slightly off balance. The action caused him to step on a piece of old wood which broke with a resounding crack. Immediately, a gray and white rabbit broke from its cover and disappeared deeper into the brush.

"Shit," Rico spit. "Could you be any more of a klutz if you tried?" Turning away, he added, "You sure didn't inherit any of your mother's moves." Then he laughed wickedly and turning to look at the boy added, "Guess you took after your dumbass father, huh?"

Hurt by the comment, but happy to see the animal's escape from death, Mitch's mouth turned up in a slight grin. Trying to sound as sincere as he could while laughing on the inside, he muttered, "Sorry, Rico. I didn't realize that you had stopped."

With an angry shake of his head and a few more derogatory mutterings, the man strode off heedless of the noise he was making as he moved through the brush. Mitch watched him go down the animal trail for a few seconds before following. He thought it was funny that no self-respecting animal could be anywhere near them with all the commotion the man mountain was making. Suddenly more nervous about the possibility of becoming lost in the forest alone than by the repugnant need to be near the man, he sped up. After walking for another half hour, the boy almost wished that the big man would shoot something – anything - so that they could just return to camp and the warm fire. Suddenly, he heard a whine come from off to his left.

"A dog? What's a dog doing out here?" he wondered aloud.

Squinting through the raindrops, he could just make out small movements in the foliage a few yards away. The sound of muted whimpering reached his ears. Mitch turned to see how far off Rico had gotten before he began to move in the direction of the sounds. Moving as quietly as possible, he pushed through the brush until he came upon what looked to be a wounded dog.

"Oh, you poor thing," Mitch uttered. "Looks like you're hurt really badly."

The animal was bleeding badly from an open gash on its flank. The boy slowly moved forward, whispering soothingly as he approached, but when he started to reach his hand out to pet it, the beast growled at him threateningly. Dropping his head back in the wet leaves, it remained lying in place.

"It's okay, boy. I'm not gonna hurt you," he said gently. The animal seemed to quiet down and closed its eyes. Mitch took the opportunity to lean forward again to pet it. Maybe he could convince Rico to help him take the dog back to camp. Then they could take it home and hopefully his mom would let him keep it! He'd been asking for a dog to keep him company at night for a long time.

"Get back from there, you dumbass!" Rico shouted suddenly making Mitch jump. Frowning, the boy turned to look at the man and saw that he was pointing his rifle at the injured animal.

"Stop! Don't shoot it!" he screamed. "He's hurt!"

"It's a wolf, you stupid little shit," Rico yelled back, "and a wounded one at that. Get outta the way before it takes a bite outta you!"

Just as Mitch was processing what Rico had told him, a flash of silver fur came flying from out of the shadows at the big man's left and bit down hard on the arm holding the rifle. The force of the wolf's leap and subsequent attack caused Rico to drop the gun and fall heavily to the ground. Immediately, he started screaming in pain as the huge animal ripped through the fabric of his coat and into the flesh of his arm. Blood and tissue went flying from the attack and covered Mitch's face and clothing where he still sat in shock next to the injured wolf. The man reached up and grabbed the big wolf by the thick fur on either side of its chest to try to push it off of him, but the blood from his wounds covering the thick fur kept him from getting a good hold. He was barely able to prevent the snapping jaws from reaching his face by placing his right forearm across the massive chest.

Suddenly, a second wolf with an oddly notched ear pounced on the man legs and sank its teeth into his vulnerable groin. Rico immediately released the alpha wolf and tried to pull the newest offender off. Unfortunately, his action allowed the massive wolf the opportunity he had been waiting for, and within seconds he had viciously torn out the man's throat. Hot blood showered down on both the dying man and the attacking wolves as Mitch watched in frozen horror. Hot tears rolled unchecked down his cheeks and he sobbed loudly. Fearing that the animals would now turn on him, he realized that he needed to try to move as far away as possible before they finished with the dead man. He turned to move slowly away from the scene when he spied the abandoned rifle lying in the dirt. Even though he had never fired a gun in his life, Mitch believed it was his only chance. He rose up on his knees and reached very carefully for the discarded rifle. His movement only attracted the attention of the alpha that turned a gore-covered muzzle in the direction of the boy and growled threateningly.

Pure contempt radiated from the wolf's ice blue eyes as he watched the boy and continued to snarl showing his sharp teeth. Mitch's fear caused him to panic. He lurched back in an effort to escape the carnage taking place a scant few feet away, but when he reached out with his hand to break his fall, it unfortunately landed very near the bullet hole on the hip of the injured wolf. The sudden weight on the festering wound caused the wolf to howl in agony. Mitch immediately jerked his hand away, but it was already too late.

The alpha male took two steps away from the dead man before leaping onto the young boy and knocking him flat on his back in the process. With its large paws standing on either side of Mitch's chest, the heavy weight of the wolf made breathing difficult for the boy, but it was those two inch long teeth in the bloody open maw above his face that terrified him the most. The big wolf's saliva dripped onto his cheek and mixed with his own tears. The wolf leaned in close and smelled at the side of Mitch's neck and the boy whimpered.

It was in that instant that Mitch knew he was going to die. He would never see his home and friends again. Never get to see another Broncos game. His last thought was of his mother. She would be alone again. Never again would he be there to brush her soft hair or to return her tender kiss. This thought caused his breath to hitch and as it did, the big wolf sank its teeth into the boy's tender neck. As the life leaked out of the boy, the wolf climbed off licking the hot blood from the fur around its mouth and walked past the cooling remains of Rico. He paused only long enough to release a hot stream of urine onto the ravaged corpse. Then he trotted up and rejoined the rest of the pack for their trek back to the wolf den. The injured male slowly stood on shaky legs and followed.

Chapter Six

January 20th
Southeast Colorado

The first day of traveling had been uneventful. Becca had made good time reaching Raton, New Mexico at just after six that night. Today she was on the final leg of her journey and knew she should be at the ranch by that evening. Grey clouds heavy with snow hung low over the mountains like sacks of wet rags, but nothing had started falling yet. As she drove through the foothills towards the mountains, she marveled at the pristine beauty of the landscape. It was like something off a Christmas card with snow dusting the fields and towns as if they had been sprinkled with powdered sugar. To Becca, it was like she was seeing it for the first time, and she could feel the stress she had been holding inside since her journey began start to drain from her body. She had been on the road for several hours and felt the desire to stop and really take in the view. Outside of Alamosa, Becca pulled the Jeep off the road onto a gravel turnout and got out of the car. Sadie was delighted with her unexpected freedom and ran from tree to bush to fence post checking out the local smells. Relishing a huge stretch, Becca was content to lean against the car and take long deep breaths of the freezing air. The pastoral beauty surrounding her seemed to wrap itself around her like a down blanket. She closed her eyes and simply let herself simply absorb the moment.

Twenty minutes later Becca had finally managed to corral Sadie back into the car and pulled back on the empty highway. She felt rejuvenated and was somewhat surprised to find that she was actually looking forward to seeing more. Maybe this trip wouldn't be as bad as she had been expecting, but only time would tell. There were still the issues of her mother's funeral and the tedious legal details that needed to be dealt with. Becca had to admit that she wasn't looking forward to either one.

The miles rolled by as she passed through the towns and images of her childhood. South Fork and the Masonic bingo hall where she and her mother would go on Saturday nights to win coupons for the local Sonic and jars of mountain honey, Wagon Wheel Gap where she was treated to a sighting of a white tailed doe and her fawn bounding through a field, crossing the Rio Grande river where she and her father had always enjoyed fly fishing for Rainbow Trout. Before she knew it, the majestic Rockies were surrounding her and she was approaching the small silver mining town of Creede, Colorado. This had been her favorite destination growing up. She had always loved shopping for treasures at the General Store and watching the tourists get excited over the fishing gear and hand sewn moccasins for sale inside the Ramble House. They were fascinated by the trophies of a noble Big Horn sheep, a fierce looking mountain lion, and record setting trout that had been caught in the area and were mounted on the wall. A plethora of photos showing proud fishermen and hunters with their trophies covered every square inch of available wall space. The only thing that had changed here in years was the personnel. Although Major Hedison still owned the store, at 91 years he rarely came in anymore. It was his eldest son, David, who now acted as proprietor and expert guide for tourists. During the summer, there was no shortage of college students looking to work in the little store, enjoying their time in the small town and the mountains surrounding it. However, tourism during the winter was nearly non-existent, so Dave and his wife were able to easily handle what little business came in to browse.

The small mining town was full of one-of-a-kind shops and even boasted a theater where a small repertory theater group would come every summer to perform, but Becca's fondest memory was of sharing a frosted mug of sarsaparilla (root beer) with her father in the Golden Nugget Saloon every time they made a trip into town. The historic bar sat on the actual site of Ford's Exchange which had been owned by the outlaw Bob Ford. Ford was famous as the man who reputedly shot Jesse James in the back and who was later killed himself by two blasts of a sawed off shotgun. Payback's a bitch, as they say. Not long after, a more permanent structure was built on the site serving hard liquor and a variety of painted ladies entertained the miners. Her father was always so proud to tell her how the gilt mirror that now hangs in the main dining room at the Silver Dollar Ranch had once hung behind the bar of the Nugget and quite possibly witnessed Jesse James' demise.

A sudden impatient honking roused her out of her nostalgia. Surprised, she realized that the traffic light she had been sitting at had turned green and a line of cars had built up behind her.

Yes, even in a town of almost 300 people, traffic still seemed to be a problem. With a wry smile on her lips, but wanting to get out of the way of the angry drivers as quickly as possible, she turned the Jeep into the parking lot of the Snowshoe Restaurant and Lodge. A growling from her stomach reminded her that she hadn't eaten anything since grabbing a complimentary donut at the hotel that morning, and knowing she still had another two hours to go, Becca thought grabbing a bite to eat was an excellent idea. Besides, if the weather turned worse like the weathermen were predicting, she felt like relaxing over a hot meal now sounded like a plan. She took Sadie to the little strip of grass beside the parking lot to let her take care of her business and then filled her bowl with fresh water. Once her thirst was quenched, Sadie jumped back in the car and stretched out on the sun-warmed back seat for a nap while Becca went into the restaurant.

The smells wafting from the kitchen were heavenly, and Becca hastily moved to an empty booth by the front windows. After enjoying a lunch of a Snowshoe burger and chili cheese fries, Becca decided she should make one last stop at the local grocery store for supplies and to top off her tank with gas. She honestly had no idea what she would find at the house once she arrived and she definitely didn't want to get caught low on gas in the mountains with a storm moving in. Grabbing a few essentials – gas, coffee, non-dairy creamer, bread, frankfurters, peanut butter, mustard, and her own personal vice, powdered sugar donuts – Becca was back on the road again within fifteen minutes for the last leg of her trip. Unbelievably, she was actually starting to enjoy the trip and was looking forward to some down time on the ranch.

The frigid wind whipped the falling snow mercilessly in and around the lair without pause. Four of the wolves were huddled in a tight mound of bodies in order to conserve as much body heat as possible, while the injured male lay slightly separate from the rest of the pack, continuously whimpering in pain. Over the past two days, his wound had begun to fester with infection and even though he continuously licked the sight where the bullet had entered his body, the noxious smell of decaying flesh was present and a greenish-yellow pus oozed out endlessly. He had weakened considerably, both from a lack of food and from the heat stemming from the infection.

The other wolves could sense that he wouldn't live much longer, and were growing more and more uneasy to be near him.

As the largest, the alpha male had stationed himself nearest the den opening to try to block as much of the cold wind from entering their lair as possible. The weather front that he had sensed was coming all day had finally come through and the high winds, ice and snow had been falling heavily. None of pack had been able to go out and hunt for food. The rabbit they had eaten a week ago had done little to satisfy their overwhelming hunger, and the alpha knew it was highly unlikely that they would be successful in their search for food anytime soon. All potential prey would be huddled in their dens until the storm had moved on. In order for their bodies to fight against the frigid temperatures, their metabolism had to use what body fat they had already stored up after killing the man to stay warm. Now the alpha instinctively realized that not only were the wolves freezing, but in all likelihood would slowly starve to death if something wasn't done.

Suddenly, Notch-Ear, the younger male, began emitting a low menacing growl. His teeth unnaturally white in the murky den. Next to him, the younger female also began to complain.

The pack leader raised his big head and looked at them sullenly. They were both immature, and he knew that they weren't strong enough to resist starvation for very long. When both of the younger wolves began to slowly crawl across the dirt floor of the den continuously moving closer to the whining wolf in their midst, the big gray understood their need. They were all starving and the smell of blood and festering meat from the injured wolf's wound was drawing them like honey to a bear. Saliva was suddenly dripping from the leader's mouth as well, and he stood up.

The wounded wolf was near delirious with pain, so he didn't immediately notice the other wolves as they began to crowd around him. However, when Notch-Ear bit hard into the injured leg, he cried out and desperately tried to kick out his other leg to break the wolf's hold on him. Unfortunately, he was just too weak for his efforts to do any good. The two females soon joined in the carnage as the alpha approached. The dying wolf no longer cried out, but looked up at the big wolf before closing his eyes as if understanding the need of the pack and granting his final permission. Without further hesitation, the big gray wolf bit deeply into the male's throat killing him quickly and greedily fed on the warm blood.

Eating one of their own kind wasn't unheard of, but very rarely happened. However, starvation is a strong motivator and their natural need to feed took over their clan mentality completely.

Not much remained of the wolf once the feeding frenzy was done - just some fur, a few bones and the little bit of blood that was already soaking into the dirt. The remaining members of the pack lay back and lazily licked at the gore that covered their coats not wanting to miss a single morsel of their meal. Their stomachs were full and distended after eating their companion. There was no feeling of remorse or shame – animals don't share that human characteristic – just satisfaction. They had simply followed their natural instincts.

Chapter Seven

Snow had begun falling as she left the grocery store with her purchases. Not too heavily yet, but certainly concerning, especially for someone who wasn't used to driving in it. The Jeep took the roads without any issue though, and Becca turned the wipers up full. She had bought the car in Dallas more for the feeling of power the big SUV gave her when sitting behind the wheel. Now she was also grateful that she had allowed the salesman to talk her into the full package including the 4-wheel drive, anti-lock brakes, and especially the heated seats. Sensing her owner's increasing tension as the snow intensified, Sadie sat up and stuck her sleek black head between the front seats for Becca to scratch.

"Don't worry, girl," she said soothingly as she rubbed the pups head. "It won't be much longer now and we'll be home in front of a blazing fire."

There was very little traffic on the roads once she was out of town, so more childhood memories came flooding back as she drove. She hadn't realized how far she had pushed them down inside years ago, but suddenly they were back as she passed by familiar landmarks. Broad Acres Ranch, the prime fishing holes along the restless Rio Grande River that she and her father had found together, the Little Dude guest ranch where her best friend had worked every summer, Freeman's General Store, and the beautiful crystalline water of Lake Cristobel. Always climbing in altitude, it wouldn't be much longer before she reached the Continental Divide and would begin her descent down the other side of the mountain on the final stretch to the ranch and her ultimate destination.

Suddenly, there was a sharp bang from the engine and the Jeep shuttered. Smoke began rising from under the hood and she lost all power. Aiming the floundering auto toward the side of the road, Becca rolled to a stop and engaged the safety brake. Although she had grown up a tomboy, auto mechanics was something she had never had any interest in, and so she had absolutely no idea what could have gone wrong or what to do about it. She could change a tire and check the windshield washer fluid, but that was the extent of her automobile knowledge.

"Crap!" she hissed and hit the steering wheel with the heels of her hands. She turned on her emergency signal and looked into the rear view mirror directly into the soulful eyes of Sadie. Shrugging her shoulders and smiling apologetically, she said, "Sorry, girl. I have no idea what to do. Guess we'll just have to wait on some Good Samaritan to come by and help us out."

The big dog wagged her tail and bumped Becca's hand with her head as if to reassure her that everything was going to be okay. Becca wished she shared the same optimism as the big lab, but she suddenly realized that they hadn't seen another car pass by for at least thirty minutes. What would she do if no one came by? The snow was really coming down heavily now and she knew she couldn't stay in the car without heat for long.

"I'll give it half an hour to see if anybody comes by," she thought. Pulling on her coat and gloves, she sat back and watched her windshield get covered by a blanket of the white powder and thin coating of ice. When there had been no other traffic for forty-five minutes, Becca had to admit that she needed to do something. Time was running out. Taking her cell phone out of her purse, she punched in 911 and waited. After a number of rings, the line was finally picked up. Becca listened to the recorded message telling her that due to the inclement weather, there would be a wait and to please be patient. The frigid temperature was really starting to seep into her bones. Finally, a young woman came on the line and Becca explained her situation. After a brief pause, the operator told her that because of the bad weather moving into the region, an eighteen wheeler had overturned on the highway causing major problems, and that in a preemptive effort by the highway department, all mountain passes had been closed in advance of the deteriorating weather front. No immediate help would be coming.

Becca couldn't believe what she was being told. Anger, frustration and even a little bit of fear tainted the tone of her response to the dispatcher.

"Then what exactly do you propose I do! I certainly don't want to sit here and freeze to death," she cried. "I need help now!"

"I understand, miss, and I'm very sorry that I can't be of more help to you. Let me transfer you to the nearest forest ranger station in that area and see if there is someone there who is in a better position to come help. Hold on, please."

"Ranger station?" Becca thought to herself. "Unless I'm suddenly attacked by angry chipmunks, what good are they going to do?" Panic was beginning to tighten its grip as she looked out at nothing, but thick woods and a curtain of heavy snow. After what was only a minute or two, but seemed like hours to Becca, she heard a few clicks and a deep male voice came on the line.

'Hello, ma'am, my name is Ben. I'm a forest ranger with the National Parks Service. I understand that you've had some car trouble. Is that right?"

His calm, melodious voice was meant to soothe her anxiety, but all it managed to do was infuriate her further. Frankly, she was scared to death and she just wanted out of here.

"Yes! My car has completely died. I have no heat, it looks like snowmagedon is coming down outside, and I've been told that I can't count on any help from the highway patrol. So, you are pretty much my last hope of getting out of here before I become a human Popsicle!

Although she was trying to keep the panic out of her voice, she realized she was failing miserably.

"Yes, ma'am. I'm going to help you, but I need to get some information from you first. Okay?"

In a gargantuan effort to calm down, Becca took a deep breath and let it out very slowly. "Sorry, what do you need from me?"

"Let's start with your name," he asked.

"My name is Rebecca Thornton. I was on my way to the Silver Dollar Ranch on the far side of the Continental Divide when something happened to my car's engine. There was a sudden loud bang from the engine, all power suddenly stopped and grey smoke started coming out from under the hood. I've been sitting here now for more than an hour and a half watching the snow slowly cover my car's windshield, the battery on my cell phone is about to die, and I'm really close to losing it entirely, so can we please hurry this up and get somebody out here to help me?"

Without any obvious reaction to her tirade, the ranger asked "From where you are now, can you see any mile marker? That will help me to locate you."

"I can't see anything for the blizzard out there. I'll have to get out of my car," she responded. "Hold on."

The door had iced up during the time Becca had been waiting for help and she had to throw all of her weight against it so she could get out. The wind whipped violently around her pulling at her coat and hair with its invisible fingers. The flying snow pelted her exposed skin and stung like hundreds of bees. Holding onto her cell phone tightly, she walked about a hundred feet in front of her car and brushed the ice off the highway marker.

"I can't read it because it's all rusted over. All I know for sure is that I had just crossed over Continental Divide on state highway 149 from Creede when it happened. Is that helpful at all?' Becca asked.

"Yes, ma'am. That gives me a much clearer idea of where you're are," the deep voice replied and it made Becca wonder if the person on the other end of the line might look as hot as his voice sounded. She listened to a rustling of papers and after a slight pause, he said "Okay, I have some good news and I have some bad news."

Becca rolled her eyes and said, "Great, as if things aren't bad enough. What's the bad news?"

"Well," he started, "The bad news is that I'm not able to leave to come get you. Federal regulations require that a ranger be on duty at all times to handle any radio emergencies, and unfortunately, I am the only one here at the moment."

Grimacing, Becca asked, "And the good news? And Mr. Ranger, it had better be some really good news, because I've been standing here in the snow for a while now, and my feet have just about become frozen to the road."

Smiling at the young lady's sense of humor in the face of her personal disaster, he said, "It's Ben, please. The good news is that there is an emergency shelter not far from where you are. I won't go into a lot of details right now, because the current storm is predicted to only be the first in a long line of fronts and the weather will only continue to worsen. You need to get to the shelter before the full force of the main front arrives. So, this is what I need you to do." He paused at this point, and then began again speaking clearly and very slowly so Becca would understand and, hopefully, remember each step.

"Now, please go back to your car and gather up whatever you feel like you might need for the next couple of days. If you have any food with you, I definitely suggest that you take it along."

"Couple of days? Wha..." she started to ask, but was cut off as Ben interrupted.

"There really isn't much time, but believe me when I tell you I will explain everything to your satisfaction once you are safely inside the cabin. Okay?"

A violent shiver that was not entirely caused by the cold ran through her, so she replied quickly, "Okay. Go on."

"Once you have everything you think you might need and can carry, I want you to start walking back down the road about a mile or so depending on where your car actually broke down. You will eventually come to a gravel road off to your left that will lead directly into the forest. If the road is already covered by the snow, you will still be able to locate it because there will be a large neon orange metal sign attached to one of the trees at the beginning of the road that reads "National Forest Service," he told her.

"Okay," Becca asked. "Then what?"

Ben smiled to himself. "This is one tough lady," he thought, but answered her with, "Just follow that road through the trees and it will open up into a meadow with a small lake in the center. Straight ahead of you, you will see the log cabin."

He paused before asking, "Got that so far?"

"Well, I'm no Danielle Boone, but I'm pretty sure I can follow a road okay. What do I do once I get to the cabin? Will it be open?"

With a small laugh, Ben replied, "No, ma'am. It has a 4 digit electronic access code that you will need to punch in to unlock the door. The code is 5 – 3 – 6 – 9 - #. Can you remember that?" This was the tricky part, because if she forgot the code and couldn't gain access to the cabin, in all likelihood, she would die of hypothermia before anyone could reach her.

Lines creased her forehead as Becca concentrated. "I think so," she said. "5 – 3 – 6 - 9 - #. Is that right?"

"Perfect," Ben replied. "Now go on and get started. Once you're inside the cabin, you'll see a red phone on the wall by the door. It's an emergency phone that's connected directly to this station. Just pick it up and push the button. I'll be here waiting for your call and then we'll go over everything else in more detail. Okay?"

"Got it. I'll call you as soon as I get inside." She disconnected the call without waiting for a reply and hurried back to get what she thought she might need from the car. She took the time to put on a second sweater under her coat, the knit hat her friend Rosemary had made as a going away gift and then tied a wool scarf over the top to cover her ears. Not the most fashionable of statements by any means, but it would keep her warm. At least for as long as it would take her to walk to the cabin, she hoped. Dumping everything out of her large shoulder bag onto the seat beside her, she proceeded to put all the groceries she could carry along with a few bottles of water inside and got back out of the car. Grabbing a flashlight from the glove compartment, her small travel bag, Sadie's blanket, the shoulder bag, and with a very excited Sadie in tow, Becca began the longest – and coldest - walk of her life.

With the wind buffeting her incessantly, it took nearly ten minutes of struggling through the falling snow with her bags and Sadie before she located the marked drive. Although she wasn't keen on entering the dark woods, she knew that at this point, she had no other choice. Colorado winters are harsh, and this particular storm looked to be completely unforgiving. She realized that she needed to find the promised shelter – and soon!

The snow on the ground inside the forest was much less as the trees helped to block the worst of the wind, but their limbs were sagging heavily under the weight of what snow had already fallen and it was much darker under the canopy. Becca paused only long enough to turn on the flashlight. Thankful that the batteries were still strong, she adjusted the bags so that they set more comfortably on her shoulders and began to move forward. Sadie was much more subdued while in the trees, nervously searching the unfamiliar area around them, and stayed close to her mistress' side no longer pulling on the leash with excitement. After another five minutes of walking through the ever deepening drifts, the gloomy forest fell back to reveal a large open area. Becca assumed this must be the meadow she was told to expect, although it was all but invisible through the falling snow and ice. At the far end she could just make out the small lake Ben had mentioned in his brief description, its surface churning with hundreds of small whitecaps whipped up like meringue by the wind. To her immense relief, she also spotted a small log cabin nestled at the very edge of the forest about a half a mile further on and not a moment too soon. All of Becca's exposed skin was now chapped and raw from the elements, and even though she was wearing gloves, she could barely feel her fingers. Sadie was visibly shaking, and her beautiful black coat, now nearly white from the blowing snow, was no match for such frigid weather. Becca knew she had to get them both inside the shelter immediately. Squinting against the bitter wind and darkening skies, they moved ahead.

Finally reaching the steps of the cabin, Becca had a momentary panic when she thought she couldn't remember the code to open the door. In fact, it took her two tries, but not because she had forgotten the sequence. Sadie stared up at her and whined, her discomfort clearly visible. Becca realized that her gloves were simply making her much too clumsy, so she reluctantly removed one in order to press the buttons. With a small click, the lock disengaged and the frosted pair finally entered the safety of the cabin.

Chapter Eight

January 20th
Southeastern Colorado

A deep blanket of snow had fallen the previous night silencing the normal sounds of the forest as though the world had been packed in cotton. The wolf pack instinctively snuggled closer together for warmth throughout the night. In the morning, the alpha left the sanctuary of the den and stretched languidly as he scented the icy air around the den. He would need to go hunting again soon, but first he went to a nearby tree and urinated, the strong yellow stream raising steam as it hit the cold white bark of the Aspen tree. The brook was now completely frozen over, and all the big wolf could do was lick at the ice. The other wolves had slowly followed him out of the den and were all waiting to see what he was going to do next. Without hesitation, the alpha turned and began trotting through the forest towards the small lake that lay within a nearby meadow. The rest of the pack followed closely behind, but when they reached the edge of the woods, they all stopped just inside the shadow of the tree line. If nothing else, the episode with the miners had taught them to use caution whenever they traveled as a group.

Ice had also begun to form along the edges of the lake and it cracked when he stepped on it. Sensing no immediate danger nearby, the big gray began to drink. The frigid water felt good and it soothed his throat as he swallowed. Sensing another presence come up beside him, he turned his head to see that his mate had joined him, but before drinking, the she-wolf rubbed her cinnamon-colored head affectionately against his shoulder. He stayed beside her as she drank, his ice blue eyes constantly surveying the forest around him for any movement that could mean a meal for the pack.

Gradually, the rest of the pack joined them at the lake's edge and drank from the icy water. With their thirst quenched, the wolves spread out exploring the surrounding area for any possibility of small game, not necessarily to eat, but for sport. Notch-Ear and the young female began wrestling in the snow pack, playfully growling and nipping at one another.

The younger male had gotten his nickname because he was missing a large piece of one ear.

That had been the price he had paid when he challenged the big grey for dominance of the pack once before and lost a piece of himself in the process. He had not challenged since, but the leader of the pack knew it would happen again at some point, especially now that they were the only two males left in the group. The senior grey gave a sharp yap to the rest of the pack warning them to stay close to the lake, and then he bounded off into the woods.

Sometime later, he came across a series of small tracks in the snow. He didn't know what type of animal had made them, and at this point it really didn't matter. Whatever it was would be food for the pack. After twenty minutes of following the tracks, a sudden movement to his right caught his attention. Freezing where he was, his cold eyes focused on the area like lasers. Several seconds later, his vigilance was rewarded when a fat opossum can waddling out from between a thick grove of birch and aspens. The alpha lowered his head, never taking his eyes off the animal, and waiting several more seconds before creeping forward. Just as he prepared to leap, the beta came flying through the air from behind him landing directly on the opossum. In the way of possums, the animal immediately rolled over on its back and played dead. Notch-Ear continued to paw at it and push it with its nose, not understanding why the creature was no longer moving. The alpha approached the scene cautiously and stopped immediately when the beta bared its teeth and growled at him. The big gray was content to simply lie down, watch and wait.

After several frustrating minutes with no success, Notch-Ear moved a few steps away and also lay down. He was panting heavily from his exertions, his breath coming out in frosty white puffs. The big gray had not moved during the whole episode, and he didn't now, but he never took his eyes away from the opossum. Notch-Ear instinctively looked at the alpha and waited for him to react. A few minutes later, a sudden alertness in the big wolf's demeanor occurred and his muscles visibly twitched causing the beta to tense up with renewed excitement, although he didn't understand exactly why.

The opossum had not felt or heard any movement in several minutes and was beginning to relax thinking that the immediate danger from his attacker had passed. In doing so, his right front foot had flexed slightly. The alpha had noticed the movement and was instantly alert, but still made no move toward the animal. Another minute passed in silence, and suddenly the opossum rolled over in preparation to run. The unexpected action startled Notch-Ear momentarily, but the big gray had already jumped forward. Determined not to miss this kill, Notch-Ear had also leapt towards the prey, but only succeeded in knocking into the big grey causing the pair to momentarily lose focus. Sensing his opportunity, the opossum quickly escaped down a nearby hole. Snarling over the loss of prey, the big wolf instantly turned and seized Notch-Ear by the back of the neck. Before he could get a good grip, the younger wolf rolled away and charged the alpha. The pair grappled for better attack positions, while continuously taking small nips at each other. After a time, the leader managed to grab hold of Notch-Ear by the throat. The action wasn't intended to kill the usurper, but merely to reinforce the big grey's position as alpha. Realizing that he couldn't escape the deadly grip of the larger wolf, Notch-Ear forced himself to go limp and exposed his belly, expressing surrender to the victor. The pair remained in that position for several more minutes before the young wolf was finally released and they began moving away together in the direction of the den. As if wanting to emphasize his dominance, periodically the alpha would turn and growl a warning at the younger male. Eventually, Notch-Ear backed off and trotted some distance behind the big gray.

Sensing the tension between the two males when they returned, the other wolves remained silent, but warily watched the duo. It had been three days since the pack had last eaten their pack mate, and the available food supply in the surrounding area would only become scarcer as the weather deteriorated. Without food, the wolves' situation would become even more desperate.

The main room of the log cabin was compact, but functional. A massive fieldstone fireplace took up one entire side of the main room. Across from it sat an old couch and a battered end table that held a kerosene lamp. The floor was made of wooden planks worn smooth from years of wear and was covered by a worn braided rug in tones of brown and gold that reached from the couch to the stone hearth. To the right of the door as you came in was a small square pine table with two chairs on one side and a matching bench seat along the wall. Just past the table and chairs was a small kitchen area, although kitchen might be too generous a description. It was more of an alcove that held a

Formica countertop, a few handmade shelves, and a steel sink with a hand pump. Nothing that you would see in Better Homes and Gardens, but the sink was clean and the cupboards were stocked with dishes and cups.

To the left of the main room, a door opened into the bunk room with enough beds to comfortably sleep six people, the mattresses rolled up and sitting atop each bunk. A second kerosene lamp sat on a table situated between two of the bunks. On the wall opposite the bunkbeds was a stainless steel case similar to those you see in the back of some pick-up trucks, though much larger in size. Several iron hooks had been screwed into the wall near the door for holding coats and other clothing.

Another door stood next to the kitchen counter, but Becca ignored it for now. She had just spotted the satellite phone on the wall next to the front door, her only connection to the outside world, and she was anxious to reconnect with the ranger.

Crossing to the phone, Becca could hear sleet pecking at the roof like a flock of hungry woodpeckers and she shivered inside her coat. Picking up the handset and she pressed the red button in the center of the phone and was rewarded with an odd, tinny sound from the other end. Ben picked up on the second ring.

"You made it!" he said cheerily. Becca noticed he was still using his professional voice, but there was a hint of something else in the question. Was it concern for her?

"Yes, we're here and so grateful to finally be out of the weather. It's sleeting here now."

"We're here? Is someone else traveling with you?" Ben asked. She suddenly realized that she hadn't told him about Sadie and she tingled slightly at the way he actually sounded disappointed by the news that there could be someone traveling with her.

With a chuckle, she said, "I guess I forgot to mention it while I was standing out in the snow freezing to death, but I have my constant companion, Sadie, with me." After a short pregnant pause, she added, "Sadie's my black lab."

Joining in the laughter, Ben acknowledged her confession with, "That's great. You'll have company while you're on vacation."

"Speaking of that," Becca queried. "Why did you tell me to bring what I might need for two or more days? Surely I won't be stuck here that long." At least she sincerely hoped not!

Serious again, Ben said, "Actually it's possible that you could be there for several days if the weather report we've received stays true. This storm is predicted to drop anything from three feet of snow in the valley to five or more feet in the mountains. Unfortunately, it could be a while before anyone will be able to reach you."

Shocked by the devastating news, Becca was beginning to realize just how lucky she had been to find this shelter.

Trying to keep the conversation light and not let on how nervous she really was, she said, "I don't think I have enough peanut butter to last that long". Her voice cracked slightly at the end giving away the tenuous façade. She actually felt like crying. This was her worst nightmare come true. Not only was she literally stuck in Colorado for the foreseeable future thanks to her mother and an unreliable car, but now she also had to deal with enough snow to bury her forever!

"Not to worry," Ben said. "I've got you covered. Before I get into all that, though, you should probably go ahead and light a fire so you can get some heat going. The wood stack in the hearth is ready to go, so all you need to do is light it. You'll find some paper in the box below the bookshelf and a box of matches on the mantle. I'll hold on while you get it lit."

Realizing she was still wearing her heavy coat and things, Becca thought that a fire sounded like a wonderful idea, so she put the phone down and did what she needed to get things started. As soon as the flames were visible among the dry wood and kindling, she returned to the phone. Sadie immediately moved closer and laid down on the run in front of the fireplace.

"Okay, looks like things will be heating up shortly. What's next?"

"If you aren't already doing so, you might want to sit down for this. There's a lot to explain and it could take a little while," the ranger explained.

Becca sat down on the sofa and promptly sank into a hole in the seat cushion her descent to the floor only saved by the struts in the couch frame. Pulling herself up out of the hole took some effort and once she had extracted herself, she joked, "You could have told me the sofa was booby-trapped before I sat down."

Ben laughed and said, "Sorry about that. The furniture for the cabins was purchased several years ago and probably gets rough handled by the highway repair crews that use them."

Becca was astonished. "Do you mean there are more of these cabins around?" she asked.

"Oh, sure. About a hundred and fifty of them, in fact. They're spread all over the state on government land, although most are situated on national park land." Ben went on to explain that the government had funded the project more than a decade ago with the end goal being to set up a number of emergency shelters exactly like the one Becca was in to temporarily house stranded motorists or highway workers who might get caught in a similar situation as she was in. The cabins were maintained by the park service so that they are always ready and waiting in case of an emergency.

"That's really a great idea," Becca said. "I know I am certainly grateful for it, but I think that the powers that be might need to do a little updating of the décor."

"Yeah, I'm sorry about that. Sometimes the highway crew gets a little rowdy," Ben said apologetically. "Besides, they're only meant to be a temporary shelter. They were never meant to be in *House Beautiful*. The good news is that while they may look a little timeworn, they are still serviceable."

Becca laughed and quipped, "No worries, and I didn't mean to sound so critical. I'm actually grateful and very pleasantly surprised. Please continue with the tour, Mr. Ranger."

"Only if you call me Ben. Ranger makes me feel like I work in Jellystone Park with Yogi and Boo Boo," said and they both laughed out loud.

"Well, the bad news is that there is technically no electricity to the cabin, at least not all the time. The cabin is too isolated for power lines to be connected, and the forest canopy is so thick that the sun can only reach the cabin during certain times of the day. To rectify this problem, solar panels were installed on the roof. Unfortunately, they only generate enough power to light the flood light outside and a small light by the bathroom at night," Ben explained.

Surprised, Becca interrupted again. "Wait a minute. Did you say there's a bathroom, too?"

Chuckling, Ben sheepishly said, "Well, it's not your typical bathroom, by any means I must admit, but if you go through the door that's next to the kitchen area you'll find a short hallway that leads to a Port-o-Let. It's completely enclosed, so you don't have to worry about battling the elements or any animals. The one drawback is that there also isn't any heat to it, but at least you don't have to go outside to use the facilities." Continuing, he added, "You'll also see a cabinet in that hallway that houses emergency supplies like candles, TP, kerosene, and the like. Feel free to help yourself to whatever you might need."

Becca shook her auburn curls as she laughed, but she had to admit that she was also very impressed by the thought and planning that had gone into this project. It might not be the Hyatt, but right now it felt like a real close second to her. "I can't wait to hear what else is here," she exclaimed, and meant every word.

Ben continued, "Well, you undoubtedly saw the hand pump in the kitchen when you came in? There is a natural spring fed well under the cabin that furnishes fresh water all year long. It's drawn up by the pump so you always have access to the water, and it never freezes as the ground helps to insulate it. Oh, and don't worry. It's perfectly safe to drink and cook with. The well water gets tested every month when we re-stock the cabin to make sure it stays free of any contaminants."

"You'll find a couple of iron skillets and pots in the kitchen cupboards near the sink, but you obviously have to use the fireplace to cook anything since there isn't a stove. Have you ever cooked over an open fire, Rebecca?" Ben asked.

"It's Becca, and no, I haven't cooked anything like that except hot dogs - once," she admitted, and then added, "But I feel certain I could boil water – if I had a reason to."

"That brings me to my next bit of good news," said Ben. "If you've been inside the bunkroom, you might have noticed a large stainless steel chest against the wall." Here he seemed to pause like a magician getting ready to astound his audience by pulling a rabbit out of his hat. "Well, inside that chest is a variety of things you might find useful, not the least of which is an assortment of pre-packaged, freeze-dried and non-perishable food for your use while you're in the cabin. There are different kinds of soups, spaghetti, chili, crackers, peanut butter, macaroni and cheese, cookies, hot chocolate, coffee, honey and lots more. You'll also see that there are extra blankets for the beds and several articles of clothing in varying sizes, such as socks, sweatshirts, pants, and such. A well-stocked first aid kit is also in there. Also you'll find toothpaste and toothbrushes, in case you left yours at home."

Becca was astounded as he ticked off each item. She could almost envision him counting each finger as he went down the list. By the end, she was literally laughing out loud.

"Wow, I really have to say that I'm completely blown away," she admitted.

Ben affected an announcer-type voice and said, "Those of us here at your National Park Service want to ensure you have all the comforts of home – within limits, of course!"

She continued to laugh and he joined in. "I'm almost afraid to ask, but is there anything more," Becca asked.

"Nope, that about sums it up," he responded, but then turned serious again as he added, "except to give you a little warning. Please keep in mind that you may be in a nice little cabin in a national park, but it is sitting in the middle of a very large forest which is home to many wild animals. Some of those animals can become dangerous if confronted or if they're hungry, like the mountain lion, badger, and wolves, although you don't have to worry about the bears right now. They're all in hibernation."

Swallowing the hard lump that had suddenly grown in her throat, Becca felt her original panic come back. "What should I do?" she asked.

Ben chuckled and said, "Really, you shouldn't have any problems with the wildlife at all, I feel certain. The only animals that you are likely see during the day will be no scarier than an occasional rabbit or deer, and maybe an aggressive chipmunk or two. The ones you need to stay clear of are the predators and they typically only come out after dark. So as long as you stay inside the cabin from dusk to dawn, you'll be just fine. They can't get into the cabin," he assured her.

"Good to know," Becca said with a sigh of relief.

"It gets dark earlier this time of year, especially in the woods, so I do suggest that before you get too comfortable, you go back outside and stock up on firewood to keep the cabin warm through the night before it's completely buried by the snow," the ranger added. "There are some extra logs by the fireplace, but you're definitely going to need more. You'll see the stack of cut wood from the front porch."

"Thanks, Ben, I'll do that as soon as we hang up. Can I get you to do one thing for me, though?"

"Whatever you need," he replied. Becca smiled and again as she felt that warm, tingly feeling come back.

"I need to let the people at the ranch know what's happened to me and that I won't be able to make it there tonight. I know that they are expecting me today and they'll be worried," she began. "There are several personal matters that I have to take care of there, and they need to understand the situation. With my cell phone's battery almost gone, I wouldn't want to risk it."

"You probably wouldn't be able to get a signal from where you are, anyway. If you give me the name and number of who you want me to notify, I'll call and let them know that you're fine, but unavoidably delayed. How's that sound?"

Still smiling, Becca replied, "That would be perfect. Thanks so much, Ben."

She provided him with Floyd's phone number at the ranch.

"We'll talk again tomorrow," the ranger promised and then they said goodbye.

Chapter Nine

Pulling her gloves on once more, Becca and Sadie headed outside again. The snow was still coming down heavily and Sadie immediately started chasing the big, wet flakes, barking and leaping at the bits of frozen ice. Looking to her left, Becca was just able to make out the pile of neatly stacked logs about seventy-five feet away from the cabin, standing just at the edge of the forest. Walking carefully down the icy steps, she was taken totally by surprise when she stepped down and sank about four inches into the mantle of white. Thankful that she had chosen to wear her boots today, she continued the trek toward her destination as quickly as she could.

Sadie had never really experienced snow like this before. What little precipitation fell in Dallas typically melted almost immediately upon hitting the ground, so this was something entirely new to her. As Becca walked over to the wood pile, Sadie darted back and forth, stopping to sniff the air every so often. So many strange and interesting smells! Soon she was exploring the trunks of the nearby trees and any open areas under the boughs where the ground might have been protected from the snowfall.

With her arms loaded with firewood, Becca turned to head back to the cabin. She laughed out loud at her big baby playing gleefully in the snow.

"Well, you've become a regular snow bunny haven't you, girl?" Becca asked the pup. Sadie sat down, snow powdering her nose where she had rooted through one of the piles and her tongue lolling out the side of her mouth looking happily up at her mistress. Her tail made its own snow angel in the powder.

Suddenly, the dog's attention shifted to farther down the meadow and her body when rigid. Sadie jumped up and turned to face the lake, a low rumbling coming from deep in her throat. Looking in the direction that the dog was facing, Becca couldn't see any reason for the dog's threatening reaction, so she continued to walk back to the cabin with the load of wood in her arms. When she reached the door, she looked back to find that Sadie had not moved an inch, but at least she wasn't growling anymore.

"Come on, Sadie-girl," she said encouragingly. "I'm really cold and hungry," adding, "How about I roast some hot dogs for dinner?"

Most of the time when Becca talked to her, the words made no sense at all to Sadie, but there were a few things that she had learned early on meant special treats of some kind for her. This was one of those times. When her mistress said the words "hot dogs," she instantly recognized the words meant one of her most favorite things in the world and Sadie immediately followed Becca back into the cabin completely forgetting what had worried her before.

Some movement at the far end of the glen caught the big gray's eye and he suddenly stopped what he was doing. His ice blue eyes focused on the scene in the distance. The she-wolf came up and tried to encourage him to play with her, but he snapped sharply at her with his jaws and she quickly backed away.

Narrowing his vision, the alpha's attention remained centered at the far end of the lake where he continued to watch the activity. There was a human moving around a structure that the wolves had never noticed before, but that wasn't what had caught his immediate attention. The person had an animal with him. Instantly, the wolf was on high alert. From where he was, the big gray couldn't tell exactly what it was, only that it was large and moved easily through the snow. At one point, the creature stopped and seemed to focus in on the pack, but then the pair continued on into the building and the wolf was left perplexed by what he had seen. Always cautious, he would wait until full dark before he ventured closer.

Chapter Ten

The cabin was much warmer by the time Becca and Sadie returned and she sighed gratefully for the heat the fireplace was putting out. She put the new logs near the hearth to dry out and removed her coat and gloves. Moving to her bags, she took the one containing the food and laid everything out on the counter. Sadie followed her every move closely, licking her mouth. Becca searched the cabinets and drawers for something to hold the wieners, but found nothing that would work.

"Guess I've got to go back outside and cut a branch," she muttered to herself. "What a pain in the wazoo." Thinking she would make this a quick trip, she only pulled on her snow-dusted coat and headed to the door. Sadie was on her heels, but Becca told her to stay inside.

"I'll only be gone a second," she promised, and opened the door. The sun had dropped very low in the overcast sky and shadows were covering most of the forest and just extending over the pristine snow. Heeding Ranger Ben's warning, she was anxious to grab a green branch and get back inside the cabin. Becca walked to a nearby Birch tree and using the paring knife she had found in one of the drawers, made quick work of cutting the branch free. As she turned to go back into the cabin, she thought that she could hear the barking of dogs. Her forehead creased as she paused on the porch and scanned the area, but the snow was falling heavily and she couldn't see far at all. She suddenly felt like she was being watched and muttered to herself, "weird" as she pulled her wool coat tighter around her and re-entered the cabin. Feeling a little foolish, she turned and slid the bolt home. After all, what could hurt her here?

Sadie was happy to see her back inside and danced around her mistress excitedly, her long tongue hanging out the side of her mouth. Becca opened the package of hot dogs and skewered three on the birch branch. Holding it over the fire, they were soon spitting and sizzling, the aroma making Becca's stomach growl loudly. Once they were cooked, she carried them over to the counter. She took down a plate from the shelf above the sink and spread mustard on a piece of bread. Taking the plate over to the table, she sat down and opened a bottle of water. Becca cut up two of the wieners and put the plate on the floor for Sadie. Then she bit into her sandwich and sighed contentedly. While it wasn't the meal she had been hoping to enjoy upon reaching the ranch, the smoky flavor achieved by cooking it over the open fire made it taste absolutely delicious and she ate ravenously. Craving more, she went back and cooked two more. Taking a bite of her new sandwich, she gave Sadie a third piece.

Her hunger satiated for the time being, Becca went over to the small bookshelf to see if there was anything there that she might like to read to help her pass the time. There were a couple of Tom Clancy novels, some car magazines from 2001 and earlier, *Moby Dick* by Melville, *Call of the Wild* by Jack London, and a few old Reader's Digests, but nothing that peaked her interest, until she noticed a jigsaw puzzle. Ironically, it depicted a beach scene complete with sunbathers holding drinks with little umbrellas in them set against the backdrop of a tranquil turquoise sea, clear blue sky, and white puffy clouds.

"Literally, any port in a storm" she said out loud and dumped the puzzle pieces onto the table. Sadie settled down on her blanket in front of the hearth and laid her big head on top of her paws while Becca began working on the outside frame of the puzzle. From out of nowhere, a sudden sense of Déjà vu struck her. This had been something that she and her parents had enjoyed doing together many times during those winter blizzards when she was a child, and she remembered how much fun it was. Her mother would make them rich hot chocolate and buttered popcorn, and the three of them would spend hours in quiet companionship putting the little pieces together until the picture ultimately revealed itself. Becca smiled at the memory and her eyes glistened with unshed tears. Intent on her work, Becca barely noticed the long, mournful howl that echoed through the cold winter's night, but Sadie did. The lab jumped up and trotted to the door emitting a low throaty growl.

Becca got up from the table and walked over to the dog. Squatting down beside her, she scratched behind the big dog's ears and said gently, "It's nothing, girl. Just the wind," but just as she said it, another howl cut through the storm. Sadie growled louder, and for the first time since she had brought the lab home, Becca was uncomfortable being so close to those sharp, white teeth. She stood up slowly so as not to startle the dog, she returned to the table and watched her gentle, loving pet transform into something frightening. Although not directed at her, Becca was still shocked by the change in her usually docile pet.

Several minutes went by without any further sounds and Becca was relieved to see the tenseness leave her lab's body. Eventually Sadie trotted back to her chosen spot on the rug, made three tight circles and plopped down with a heavy sigh and a snort. Soon she was snoring loudly. Apparently, whatever real or imagined menace had been out in the storm was no longer a threat. Becca was still slightly alarmed by what had happened, however, and continued to simply stare at the black lab and wonder what had caused her to behave so completely out of character.

Looking at her watch, she was startled to see it was after eleven o'clock. Leaving the puzzle as it was, she stretched and opened the door that Ben had told her led to the toilet. Sure enough, at the end of the short hallway sat the iconic blue and white metal container normally seen around construction sights and at sporting events. A dim bulb hanging in the middle of the hallway was the only light and the thin light did little to dispel the shadows, but it was still better than no light at all. She left both the door to the cabin and to the Port-O-Let open when she went inside to relieve herself. Next time she decided that she would bring one of the kerosene lamps with her. Humming to herself, she entered the portable toilet and sat down. Humming *Piano Man* by Billy Joel, a minute or two had passed before she realized there was another sound she hadn't noticed and couldn't quite place. It was a gentle huffing, scratching sound. Could it be a weird wind draft of some kind? She didn't actually feel one, but she hadn't really looked in the hallway when first arriving, so it was certainly possible that there were gaps or holes in the wall that she had missed.

Then it hit her. Something was on the outside of the cabin trying to get in! Now that she was focusing on the noises, she could tell that something was moving along the wall, sniffing and every so often tentatively scratching at the wood, and it sounded big! Becca finished her business quickly and ran back into the cabin, shutting the connecting door with a bang. Disturbed from her slumber, Sadie looked up at her with annoyance from her place by the fire. Then with a snort, she rolled over and closed her eyes again.

There was no lock on the inside door, so Becca carried one of the wooden chairs from the table over and slid it under the door knob to secure it the only way she knew how. For good measure, she also went and made sure that she had bolted the front door. She knew that she would have to walk the perimeter to see exactly what, if anything, had been rooting around the cabin, but that was something she would wait to do in the daylight. Not in the dark and certainly not in the middle of a whiteout.

Banking the fire, she blew out one of the lamps and carried the other with her into the bunk room. Changing into her cozy, blue flannel pajamas, she felt certain that after the earlier excitement, sleep would be a long time coming tonight, but that turned out to not be the case. Lying on the soft mattress and snuggled within a warm cocoon of blankets, exhaustion overcame her and soon she was deep in a slumber.

Chapter Eleven

February 6th

The big wolf had watched the cabin for hours waiting to see if there would be any more activity, but nothing else happened. The two younger wolves had become restless and chased each other back in the direction of the den, but his mate remained close by his side. She could sense the excitement in him and made no move to leave even though it was now full dark and they should be hunting for food.

When the moon started to rise, the gray stood up and slowly trotted along the lake's shoreline, the female following closely behind. He traveled along the side of the lake opposite the cabin, but upon reaching the end closest to the building, he stopped and lay down in the snow. His gray coat having been frosted with ice worked to camouflage him in the snow. The female stopped as well, but remained standing. The gray lifted his large head and sniffed the air. Wood smoke and the scent of cooking meat reached out to him even through the snowfall, but there was also a fainter odor that was much more intoxicating and caused his body to tremble with excitement. Saliva dripped from his maw and the female whined slightly as she also recognized the scent for what it was. Still he waited. The episode with the hunter had made him overly cautious. Finally, he rose again and walked stealthily towards the cabin. The snow was now up to his massive chest and his mate was having difficulty keeping up, but in less than fifteen minutes they had reached their destination.

He mounted the steps to the porch and immediately picked up confusing scents. The canine smell was obvious, but the human scent was different than the hunter's had been. Curious, but still cautious, he left the porch and turned to follow the edge of the building. Suddenly, light flooded the area, startling the pair as the automatic flood light came on in the yard. After several seconds, the wolf dismissed the interruption and sensing no immediate danger, resumed his exploration of the structure.

His curiosity eventually waning, the big gray was preparing to enter the tree line at the rear of the building, when he heard movement coming from behind the wall. He walked slowly toward the wall and stopped. The sound of humming surprised him, and he cocked his head to the side as he stared fixedly at the wood wall. The female wolf moved up beside him, waiting to see what he was going to do. Tentatively, he reached out with one of his massive paws and scratched at the wood a few times to see if it would allow him any access. Slivers of wood came off with each swipe of his claws, and it soon became obvious that he wouldn't be getting in this way. When an owl suddenly hooted from the woods, he turned around and with the female following silently behind disappeared back into the forest.

Daylight was coming through the window blinds when Becca was suddenly awakened by Sadie licking her face. Laughing while she gently pushed the dog away, Becca said, "Okay! Okay! I'm up!"

Sadie backed off, but only far enough to allow Becca to sit up on the side of the cot and rub her face. "This must have been what Rip Van Winkle felt like after waking up twenty years later," she mumbled. "I could use a caramel latte Grande right about now."

Sadie gave a sharp bark, and Becca looked at her sweet pup. "Right, you probably need to go badly, huh? Just let me get my boots on first."

Pulling her boots on over her stockinged feet, she stood up and made her way into the main room. Grabbing her coat and gloves, she paused only long enough to add a log to the glowing embers in the fireplace. Crossing to and unlocking the front door, Becca let the lab out into the snow blanketed yard. Sadie immediately started sniffing for a suitable location to relieve herself while Becca remained on the porch, her arms wrapped tightly around her body for extra warmth. She silently wished she was still in bed under the mountain of blankets. The snow was still falling, and it looked as if another foot had fallen during the night. Looking out over the vast snow-covered field, Becca suddenly remembered the frightening experience from the night before. She carefully went down the steps and walked slowly toward the back of the cabin. Snow drifts had accumulated on the windward side of the cabin, and as she reached the back wall, she hesitated. This part of the cabin was very near the tree line and the sun didn't reach very far in. The dark shadows made her uneasy, but just then Sadie came bounding up to her with all the energy of a 2-year old. Laughing, Becca squatted on her heels and scratched behind the dog's ears while Sadie slathered her face with kisses. She relaxed knowing that if there was anything to fear, Sadie would let her know.

Continuing along the wall, she realized that not a lot of snow had accumulated on the leeward side of the building as it was more protected from the wind and within the shelter of the trees. Walking was easier there, too, and she moved much more quickly. A few feet in however, Becca froze. There in the dirt near the outside wall, she found a series of tracks that had been nearly obliterated by the falling snow. She had no experience tracking animals, and so she was at a total loss as to what could have made the tracks, but they looked like they came from a large animal as they continued through the snow and into the woods. She also noticed a few places where it appeared the wood along the cabin wall had been shredded and pieces of it still littered the ground. Suddenly, Sadie burst out of the woods and bounded ahead of her kicking up snow in her excitement. She was obviously enjoying the freedom from the cabin, and Becca couldn't help, but smile at her unrestrained enthusiasm. Picking a branch off the ground, Becca's attention returned to the tracks. To her surprise, she realized that they appeared very similar to Sadie's tracks. Looking at them more closely, she could see that while they were much larger, they looked relatively the same. Could it have been a dog trying to get into the cabin last night, maybe to escape the cold weather? Maybe that was the animal she had heard howling.

"Poor thing," she said. "I hope it's okay. Now I feel so silly about the way I reacted."

Remembering that Ben was going to call this morning and not wanting to miss her opportunity to speak to him again, she hurried back inside, the tracks forgotten for the moment.

Now that Sadie had taken care of her personal business and she was back inside the warm cabin, Becca retrieved an enamelware coffeepot from a cupboard in the kitchen, filled it with water from the pump and added some of the coffee that she had bought in town. Placing the pot on the grate in the hearth to brew, she returned to kitchen and splashed some of the freezing cold spring water onto her face. Gasping at the instantaneous sting from the frigid wake up call, Becca said, "Next time I'll heat it first". Not finding a towel handy, she decided to check the chest in the bunk room.

Lifting the heavy lid, she was amazed at the treasures she discovered inside. Grabbing a soft towel off the stack and drying her face, she began looking through the available food supplies until she came to several packages of instant oatmeal. Taking a couple out, she went back to the main room to get a pot of water boiling. She hadn't been lying to Ben when she told him she could boil water, but just barely. Cooking was certainly not one of her long suits. Not when Dallas had a multitude of various cuisine restaurants literally available for delivery any time day or night. Removing the coffeepot, she poured a cup of the rich, black liquid, being very careful to strain the grounds out as she poured, and added some of the creamer she had brought with her. As she was taking her first delicious sip, the phone buzzed.

Becca felt a thrill as she hurried over to the phone. "Geez," she thought, "I'm like a teenaged girl waiting for a call from her first boyfriend!" Picking up the receiver, she said, "Hello? Ben?"

"Good morning, Becca," said the warm, cheerful voice. "Enjoying the winter wonderland?"

"Oh, it's beautiful so long as you don't have to get out in it," she laughed. "Any word on when I'm going to be able to get out of here?"

He returned her laughter and quipped, "Sorry to hear you're not happy in the cabin, but word is that the snow is going to continue through today and tomorrow at least. Doesn't look good for rescuing damsels in distress. Sorry I don't have better news."

Disappointed by the news, Becca said, "I don't mean to complain, and the cabin is wonderful." She paused briefly before adding, "It's only that there is so much to do at the ranch and it's really frustrating to be so close and still not be able to get there."

"Someone special waiting for you there?" Ben asked, not really sure that he wanted to hear the answer.

"Oh, no. You see, I'm heading home to bury my mother and this delay is just inconvenient. That's all."

"I'm so sorry to hear that. I completely understand the urgency," Ben said sincerely, "and I promise to get you out of there as soon as I possibly can. In the meantime, I spoke with your foreman and he assured me that he has everything under control and that you shouldn't worry."

Well, at least that was something, Becca mused.

"How was your night?" the ranger asked. "Any problems?"

Taking a sip of the strong coffee, she replied, "No, everything was fine, nothing special." Then she remembered what happened and what she had found this morning. "Wait. Now that you ask, there was one strange thing that happened."

"What would that be?"

"Well, when I was getting ready to go to bed, I heard scratching from outside the little hallway and what sounded like a dog snuffling around. In fact, when I went out this morning with Sadie, I found some animal tracks that looked a lot like hers, but were almost as big as my hand. They circled the cabin and then took off into the woods. Should I be worried?"

Ben was silent for a few seconds, and then asked softly, "How did Sadie react?"

Totally oblivious to Ben's change of tone, Becca responded, "She was so excited about being out in the snow, I don't think she even saw them, but she did act funny last night." After a pause to take another sip of her coffee, she continued, "A couple of times she went to the front door and growled. She never does that and I have to say that it was a little bit scary. She just wasn't acting like the loving pup I raised. Why?"

Ben hesitated again before answering. He wasn't sure how familiar Becca was being in the wilderness and he didn't want to alarm her unnecessarily, but he had felt an instant connection with this young woman and he was surprised by how much he was starting to care about what could happen to her. What he definitely knew without a doubt was that he couldn't leave her completely unprepared. "Becca, I need you to listen to me very carefully. Okay?"

Suddenly wary of his serious tone, she quickly replied, "Of course, Ben. What is it?"

Choosing his words carefully, Ben began.

"From what you've described to me, it sounds as if you might have attracted the attention of a wolf pack that has been sighted several times in the forest during the past couple of months. In fact, a few weeks ago, a pack attacked a miner at the Puckett Silver Mine and very nearly killed him." Ben heard the sharp intake of breath from the other end of the phone line and quickly added, "Look. It's certainly possible that this isn't the same pack, but it's better to err on the side of caution in these types of situations, don't you agree?"

"Absolutely! Please, tell me what I need to do," Becca responded and cringed at the obvious trembling in her voice. She wanted to be strong, especially in front of this man, but she had been totally blindsided by this bit of news. Blindsided and terrified!

"Typically wolves won't come near where we humans are, especially during the day, but these wolves don't seem to follow the natural habits of gray wolves," Ben explained. "However, I still don't feel like you have anything to worry about during the day, especially because you have the added protection of a dog."

She huffed at the suggestion that Sadie could be anything other than the loving sidekick she'd always been and said, "I really don't know how much protection Sadie would be. She's such a gentle soul and I don't think she would ever hurt a fly. Sure she chases the occasional trespassing squirrel back home, but never with much conviction."

"You might be surprised. Dogs are often very protective of their owners. Didn't you tell me that she sensed something outside earlier in the evening?" he asked.

"Well, yes, she was growling at something, but I looked and couldn't see anything at the time."

"Believe me, Becca, dogs have a much keener sense of detection when they feel danger is nearby. Her reaction tells me that she had to know that the wolves were there and was letting them know she was there, too." Then he added, "She definitely was protecting you."

"Oh, my God!" Becca, looked over at the big lab and her eyes teared up. The dog tilted her sleek head and her chocolate brown eyes looked at her mistress as if asking if she was alright. Becca had had no idea what Sadie had been doing last night, and it had frightened her badly. Now, she understood that the hostility Sadie had shown had never been directed *at* her, but *for* her and she felt ashamed of herself.

"The main thing is that you have to be very cognizant of things that are happening around you. It would probably be best to remain inside now as much as possible until you're rescued. You have everything you need right there. Of course, I realize that there will be times when you have to go outside say for firewood, or so Sadie can take care of her business and the like, but please don't take any unnecessary risks – even in the daytime, and remember that anytime you go outside, take Sadie with you. She'll let you know if there's anything around that you might need to worry about."

Ben stopped at this point to let that last part sink in, before adding, "Becca, the rules haven't changed when it comes to being particularly cautious at night. Under no circumstances would I recommend you going out after dusk, so make sure that you have taken care of everything you need to do outside before then. I would even recommend that you leave a lamp burning all night long. Nocturnal animals tend to avoid places that are well lit, so it could help deter any nocturnal visits."

Becca sat in stunned silence. This was certainly not anything she wanted to have to deal with on top of the deteriorating weather. This whole situation was turning into her worst nightmare and she wished she could just wake up in her own bed back in Dallas. She closed her eyes and took a deep, ragged breath.

"Becca? Did you hear what I said?" Ben asked.

When she answered, her voice was barely above a whisper and she kept her eyes closed when she replied, "Yes, Ben, I understand."

Hearing the obvious fear in her response, Ben hastened to add, "Don't worry about this too much. As long as you follow the rules, you'll be just fine and I promise that I will come for you and Sadie as soon as I can. Everything will be okay. Believe me."

Becca realized she was nodding, but hadn't actually said anything back, so she simply said "Uh-huh."

"One last thing, Becca," Ben added. "Remember that this satellite phone works both ways, so anytime you feel threatened, need help, or just need to talk to someone, feel free to pick it up. The line is always open and I'll be here for you no matter what time you call."

A heavy tear ran down her cheek as Becca said, "Thanks, Ben. It does make me feel a little better to know I'm not completely cut off from civilization," she said. Saying their mutual goodbyes, Becca hung up the phone and sobbed aloud. Sadie got up at the sound and trotted over to lay her big head in the girl's lap. Absently, Becca began stroking the smooth, soft fur and the lab turned her warm gaze to look up at her mistress. Ben was right. She could do this and Sadie would be there to help her. Besides, the storm has to end soon, right?

Chapter Twelve

February 7th

The big gray paced anxiously around the outcropping that protected the den. The young ones had gone out hunting that morning, but had come back empty-handed. It was late afternoon now and they were all beginning to show signs of intense hunger after several days without food. The heavy snowfall was working against the pack by keeping all of the smaller animals cozy in their nests, and the alpha male was restless. The big grey left the relative shelter of the den and the rest of the pack behind as he moved silently through the snowy forest until he reached the tree line at the northern end of the meadow. His muscles twitched from the tension his body held, and he could hardly contain the anticipation he was feeling. He had learned the hard way that wherever there were men, there was also food, but the wooden structure at the other end of the valley was an obstacle he had never encountered before.

Then there was the bitch to contend with, as well. He knew he could take it down, but not without cost. The hound was young, energetic and would likely not back down from a fight. The pack had already lost two of its members. It could ill afford to lose any more. The alpha understood that he had to protect the remaining members at all costs, and right now food was paramount for their survival.

He turned his nose up and scented the frigid air. With a snort, he rose from the protection of his cover and began to soundlessly trot in the direction of the cabin. Following his natural instincts, he made sure to stay in the shadow of the tree line that ran parallel to the lakefront. He sensed rather than saw when his mate and the other wolves caught up with him and immediately fell into step behind. They could all feel his eagerness and while they didn't understand exactly why, their own excitement continued to build.

Not wanting to waste the tepid daylight, Becca decided to take care of what needed to be done outside as quickly as possible. The snow was falling like spun sugar now, and at any other time, she would love to simply stand and watch its beauty, but right now it felt like it was only reinforcing her prison. The snow fell continuously and continued to build higher around the cabin. The frigid North wind instantly whipped the ice crystals to bite into her skin like tiny teeth as she left the warmth and safety of the shelter. Pausing on the small front porch, her eyes swept the landscape in search of anything moving or out of place, but didn't see anything that immediately concerned her. With Sadie by her side, she carried out the small bag of trash that had collected in the kitchen out to the fire drum and dropped it in. Then she swung back by the log pile and loaded her arms with as much firewood as she could carry. Making her way through the snow pack that was now up to her knees with the heavy logs was difficult and slow-going, but she felt a sense of urgency and was happy that she was able to make it the entire trip without losing her balance and falling. She considered the adventure a real success.

As she was climbing back onto the porch, she heard honking coming from the direction of the lake and was delighted to see that a small cluster of wild ducks had landed in the only patch of deep water that had not frozen yet. "Beautiful," she said out loud, but then from of the corner of her eye, a sudden movement within the smoky shadows of the woods started warning bells going off in her head. With her heart in her throat, she stood absolutely still and watched the forest for several more minutes, but nothing else appeared. When the cold penetrated the protection of her coat and gloves, she shrugged and thinking she had simply imagined it, Becca turned to re-enter the cabin with her bundle of firewood. As she continued to climb the steps, she happened to glance at Sadie, and noticed that she had not moved an inch from her position on the porch. Her attention seemed focused entirely on the forest, her ears pricked up listening for any sound.

With another shiver, Becca scanned the stark woods once more before softly saying, "Come on, girl. It's starting to snow harder." With obvious reluctance, Sadie turned and followed her inside.

"Guess I'm more spooked than I thought I was," she decided, shaking her head from side to side. After dropping the bundle of iced logs to the floor near the fireplace, she re-stoked the dying embers and placed a pot of water on to boil. After the water had heated, she added one of the packets of vegetable beef soup that she had found in the bunk room chest and waited for it to simmer while she made herself a fresh cup of coffee. Pulling out a piece of bread, she sat down to enjoy her lunch. Sadie was watching her intently, her soft brown eyes following her every move as the spoon dipped from the steaming bowl onto her mouth and back again. Laughing, Becca took a piece of bread and dipped it in the rich broth.

"Here you go, you big beggar!" The dog took the proffered tidbit without hesitation, licked her mouth, and then immediately sat back down, obviously waiting for more. No longer able to ignore the lab's prolonged stare, Becca sighed loudly, but got up and took down a second bowl. Careful not to spill any, she poured half of the rich, red broth over some small pieces of torn bread and placed it on the floor by her pet's water bowl.

"Be careful! It's still hot," but by the time she had finished the sentence, the bowl was empty. Laughing, Becca said, "Well, I don't think I even need to wash that bowl – but I will!"

Picking up both bowls, she carried them to the sink and pulled out the metal dishpan from below the cabinet. Pouring in hot water from the pot on the fireplace, and then tempering it with cold water from the pump, Becca added soap and thoroughly washed the handful of dirty dishes. Then, picking up the dishpan, she opened the front door to throw the water out, and froze.

Moving across the porch where less than thirty minutes ago there had been just two sets of tracks – hers and Sadie's - she now found several more prints in the deep snow that covered the wooden deck. She instantly knew that the tracks she was seeing meant that the wolves had been there; she stepped back inside and slammed the door. Sliding the bolt home, Becca turned and leaned her back against the door only to find Sadie facing away from her and staring down the little hallway to the bathroom in full defense mode. The hair along her sleek black back was standing straight up and she was once again growling menacingly. Of course, there was nothing to be seen, but as Becca stood there holding the still full dishpan, she began to hear movement along the outside of the walls.

Sadie began moving very slowly, but deliberately down the hallway, her head down low as though she were tracking a chipmunk and never ceasing her throaty warning, until she reached the part of the wall near where the Port-O-Let stood. This area was not original to the cabin, but had been added specifically to allow the inclusion of the chemical toilet. There was no permanent floor here, only hard packed earth and wood shavings so that the container could be easily transported in and out of the space as necessary. The surrounding walls had concrete reinforcement along their base, but Becca had no idea how deep the concrete actually went underground. Could the wolves dig their way in? She shivered at the thought.

Sadie put her nose near the base of the wall where the outside door stood and immediately went into a barking frenzy. Periodically, she would lunge at the door, but it was securely bolted from the outside and didn't budge. Sadie's sharp teeth snapped at the invisible intruder. Suddenly, answering growls and a much more frantic scratching came from the other side of the wall, causing the startled lab to back away a few steps. Becca called for Sadie to come to her, but the dog continued to bark frantically, charging at the wall and then backing away as though challenging whatever was on the other size. Fearful that her dog would enrage the wolves enough for them to try digging in, Becca took hold of her collar and physically pulled the dog back into the main cabin closing the door to the hallway behind them. Again, she braced a wooden chair under the door. She had no idea if the barricade would be of any use should the wolves eventually find a way in, but it was the only defense she had. Distracted, Becca didn't notice the random small droplets of blood scattered on the floor.

Nearly in frenzy, Sadie began frantically running from room to room searching for the invaders, while Becca went to the phone and picked up the receiver. Pressing the red panic button, she was gratified to hear it was picked up immediately at the other end.

"Becca? What's wrong?" Ben asked her, the concern evident in his tone.

"They're back!" she screamed into the receiver. "The wolves! They're back and they're trying to get in! Oh, God, Ben, you *have* to get got me out of here!"

Ben could hear the sheer panic in her voice and knew he needed to get her to calm down. How he wished he could take her in his arms and hold her close, but wishes weren't going to help right now.

Keeping his voice even, he said "Okay, Becca, I understand that you're scared, but you've got to calm down. Believe me when I tell you that there is no way that the wolves can get into that cabin," he told her reassuringly. "The logs are much too thick. The windows are double-paned and set too high off the ground for them to reach. Just keep the doors locked and you will be fine."

Not at all pacified, she yelled into the phone, "No, God damn it! You don't understand! They aren't attacking the logs. They're trying to dig *under* the walls in the hallway! Under them!" Her tears were falling freely now, but she didn't care. Her fear was a tangible thing and she could literally feel it choking her. Her terror continued to grow as Sadie ran from room to room barking incessantly at the invisible intruders.

Ben could hear the pure fear in her voice and Sadie's warning yips, but he knew that if Becca lost total control of her emotions right now, she would never be able to deal with what she might have to face later. He realized his first priority was to calm her down quickly to keep her from doing something rash, so he was careful to choose his next words very carefully.

Drawing on his years of training, Ben managed to adopt a calmer, more professional tone before speaking again. He wasn't really concerned that the wolves would be able to breach the walls of the cabin. He knew that there was no way that they could, but they definitely posed a real danger to this woman and her pet as long as they lingered outside the cabin. He had to do his best to alleviate her fears. "Becca, listen to me. I know that you're a strong, capable woman," he told her. "You've proven that by the way you've handled this whole situation so far. Nothing has been easy for you, but you've dealt with it wonderfully. Those wolves are just another piece that has to be dealt with, and I'm confident that you can do it. I have complete and total faith in you, but you aren't in control when you panic. You have got to calm down and listen to me. Can you do that for me?"

Swallowing back her panic and biting her lip, she wiped her tears with her shirt sleeve and with a trembling voice said, "Yes, Ben, I promise I'll do my best."

Smiling once again at her strength and determination, he responded, "That's my girl." Taking a deep, breath, he continued, "Now, like I told you before, it's very unusual for wolves to come anywhere near human habitats at all, but it's incredibly rare for them to do so in the daytime. The fact that these wolves are there tells me that they must be starving and have probably followed the scent of your cooking straight to the cabin. Simply put, they are looking for food."

Ben paused to give her time to accept what he was telling her, and then continued on. "I know that you're understandably scared because you can hear them digging on the other side of the wall, but I can assure you that you don't need to be. The cement barricade you see along the walls goes down a foot into the frozen earth, so there is virtually no way that they could dig their way in to you. Okay?"

Hearing his words caused relief to immediately rush over her and she nearly cried for joy. "Oh my God, yes! That definitely makes me feel better. Thank you!"

Feeling happy that he had been able to give her the comfort she needed just then, he added, "In all likelihood, once they realize there is no ready food to be had, their need to feed will make them go back into the woods to hunt for something else to eat."

At that moment, a loud hollow thunk came from outside. "Wait a minute," Becca said. "Something's happening outside."

She set the receiver down on the end table and went to the small kitchen window to look out. Her eyes widened as she saw three wolves shredding the paper garbage sack she had taken out to the burn barrel minutes ago into pieces just so they could get to the meager scraps inside. The fire drum had been knocked onto its side and she realized that the toppling had been the source of the noise she had heard. A slight movement to the right of the frenzied wolves made her shift her gaze and she was startled by what she now saw. Standing perfectly still and looking directly at her was an enormous silver gray wolf. He didn't move a muscle, but his unusually intense blue eyes stared straight back at her. The hostility she saw burning in those eyes was like an electric shock and she staggered back from the window.

Never taking her eyes off the window, Becca picked up the phone again and stuttered, "B-Ben, please t-tell me if now that the blizzard is over we'll be able to get out of here."

A frown creased the ranger's forehead. Her tone alerted him that something else must have happened, but he decided it was better not to ask what. At least not at the moment.

Maintaining his steady tone, he replied, "The latest reports I'm seeing say that the valley roads have been cleared for traffic, but the mountain roads are still impassable and are shut down. They're hoping to get the plows out to clear them off sometime tomorrow or the next day," he told her. "So, the good news is that you could be on your way very soon."

The news that rescue could be coming soon filled Becca with hope, and turning away from the window, she responded with, "Oh, Ben. That's the sweetest thing you could have ever said to me. Thank you so much!"

Blushing, Ben cautioned, "I don't want to get your hopes up too high. A lot of things still have to fall into place before that can happen, but at least it looks promising at this point. Just hang in there a little bit longer, okay?"

"Absolutely!" she exclaimed enthusiastically. "I feel like I can definitely handle it now that I know for sure the end is truly in sight."

For his part, Ben would be sorry to say goodbye to her when this was all over, but he could certainly sympathize with why she wanted out of there so badly and he would do everything he could to make that happen for her. Hanging up the phone, Ben had only one thing on his mind. He needed to call in a favor.

Chapter Thirteen

The wolves had continued to search the area around the structure for food, but found little of interest to them. Even tipping over the burn barrel had revealed nothing that they could make a good meal from, so the two younger wolves quickly moved off to search for prey further within the forest. However, there was something that continued to entice the alpha to remain near the cabin and his mate followed closely behind. The big grey had been drawn to several places where the dog had urinated in the yard, and he made sure that he covered those areas with his own scent thereby marking his dominance to any other males in the area. The two wolves then approached the cabin with extreme caution and renewed their search for a way inside. Following the outside walls, the pair eventually came to the area where the alpha had scratched and scented on the previous night. The duo began pawing at the frozen ground gaining little ground until they heard growling coming from inside the cabin.

They paused in their digging only momentarily, before beginning again in earnest. The alpha was intent on his work, but stopped suddenly. He lifted his impressive silver head and sniffed the air. Yes, there was something here and it only made him more determined to get inside. The female also noted a change in the air, but her reaction was much more feral. She emitted a sharp bark directed toward the male who suddenly turned and snapped back at her. The female retreated slightly from the rebuff, continuing a more muted growl.

Growling from deep in his chest, he began to scratch furiously at the wooden blockade causing the pads of his feet to bleed. From inside, a more frantic growling and barking erupted, but it didn't deter him in anyway. In fact, it seemed to fuel his determination. As the alpha became more excited by what he was sensing inside, his temper turned towards his offending mate, and he snapped viciously at her again. He caused her no harm, but the female was stunned by his sudden and unexpected attack. Immediately, she backed away from the big male, and moved into the dark shelter of the trees and lay down watching and waiting to see what he would do.

The male remained in place for several more minutes as though waiting for something to happen. His muscles twitched excitedly within his body. When nothing else happened, he reluctantly retreated back into the woods. He was very hungry and he knew the others in the pack needed food, too, if they were going to survive the winter. The female came to him and rubbed her body against his to acknowledge his authority. He rewarded her with a half-hearted nip at her ear just to remind her who was in charge, and then the duo moved deeper into shadow of the forest together.

* * * * * * *

Sadie continued to act strangely and Becca grew more concerned. Her constant whining and pacing from room to room as if searching for something was starting to get on her nerves.

"She probably just needs to go out again," Becca mused, but wasn't sure that was a good idea. At this point, she had no idea where the wolves were, even though she hadn't seen or heard anything from them in the last couple of hours.

Speaking softly, she said, "Okay, Sadie-kins, I'll take you out, but you'll have to stay on the leash. I can't have you running off in the woods again."

Recognizing the word "leash," Sadie immediately ceased her keening and went to the door with her tail whipping back and forth to wait while Becca took the time to don her boots, coat and gloves. Once she had attached the leash to Sadie's collar, she opened the door as quietly as she could and surveyed the area around the cabin through the screen door. Seeing nothing of the wolves, she started to open the door, and stopped. Closing the door again, she moved back across the room and picked up the only weapon available to her – a wrought iron fireplace poker. Then she returned to the door and grabbed hold of Sadie's leash before opening the solid wooden door and pushing open the screen.

Stepping out onto the small deck took every bit of her courage she had, and she moved slowly while her eyes constantly searched around them for any signs of attack. Sadie was literally trembling with excitement, and Becca had to smile. Obviously, she needed to go very badly!

The pair moved down the steps and Becca deliberately led the hound away from the direction of the woods and into the open area at the front of the cabin. Sadie darted around as far as the restraint would allow until she finally found the spot she had apparently been looking for. While she was taking care of business, Becca continued to search the tree line for the wolves. Not seeing anything, but a couple of chipmunks scrounging for food, she began to relax until she heard Sadie's warning growl. Turning her head to see what the lab was focused on, her heart stopped when she saw a copper-colored wolf standing approximately thirty feet away with her head down and her teeth bared. Her yellow eyes were focused directly on Sadie and she was snarling threateningly. Saliva dripped from her impressive canines and Becca's heart jumped to her throat. A few feet behind the first wolf stood another that was easily twice the size of the first one. This one had silver and gray fur with eyes the color of a spring-fed lake. The head was huge, and Becca was terrified by the sheer size of him. She had seen this wolf before.

Becca had seen enough National Geographic documentaries to know that turning her back and running to the cabin would be the worst possible thing she could do at that moment even though that was exactly what her body wanted her to do. She also knew that with Sadie so focused on the wolf, it would be unlikely she would be able to persuade her to follow her in any case, but she had to do something. Slowly Becca began shortening the lead of the leash gradually pulling Sadie back to her, and it seemed to be working until the larger wolf began to move slowly forward and came to a stop in front and to the side of the smaller one. He, it was obviously the male, made no move to get any closer, but seemed content to simply stand with its legs braced. It seemed more like his goal was getting between the other two canines. At that moment, Sadie surprised Becca by doing something totally unexpected.

Chapter Fourteen

Sadie suddenly jerked forward hard on the leash, causing Becca to lose her grip on the leather strap. Immediately, the black lab took off towards the two wolves. Becca screamed for the dog to return to her, but her cries were ignored. It almost seemed like Sadie was meeting a playmate. Her tail was wagging and her tongue hung from her mouth on one side like a strip of bacon. When she was only a few feet from the big male, she stopped and proceeded to turn her backside towards him. Becca was momentarily confused, and then she realized what was happening.

"Oh, God, no!" she whispered. "She's in season!"

A lifetime ago in Dallas, Becca's vet had explained to her that it would be less traumatic on Sadie physically if she allowed the dog to go through two cycles before actually being spayed, but she hadn't been expecting it to happen again so soon. It had only been ten months ago since she came into heat for the first time, and it couldn't have picked a worse time to come back.

No wonder the male had been trying so hard to breach the cabin walls.

Still in shock by the sudden turn of events, she barely noticed when the smaller of the two wolves ran past the big male and charged at Sadie. The wolf flew onto the lab's back in a flurry of teeth, fur, and saliva. Sadie yelped in pain as the smaller wolf bit deeply into her shoulder. Instantly her shiny black coat was splattered in crimson. Waking up from her stupor and realizing that her companion was in dire trouble, Becca let loose a primal scream and raced forward without hesitation in an effort to try and rescue her dog from the vicious she-wolf. However, in focusing on the struggling pair, she completely failed to notice that the male wolf was advancing on her.

Reaching the battling animals, Becca retrieved Sadie's leash in one hand, and suddenly remembering she still carried the fireplace poker in her other, she struck the she-wolf twice in the side of her head with all of her might. The female wolf went down and didn't get back up. Becca could see that one of her strikes must have punctured the beast's left eye, because blood and ichor was now leaking from the wolf's orbital socket onto the surrounding fur. Becca loved all animals and any type of cruelty to them made her furious. Surprised and stunned by what she had done to the wolf, Becca had just taken a step back when the male wolf viciously attacked her. Sinking its teeth into the calf of Becca's left foot, she shrieked in panic. The sharp fangs easily punched through the leather of her boot to reach the tender meat underneath drawing blood. The big wolf continued to bite down and the pain from the bite was excruciating. Tears instantly began to stream down her cheeks as she cried out loud. Panicked and desperately working to escape the deadly jaws, Becca brandished the poker above her head and struck the big wolf again and again until he finally released her foot. Blood was running freely down the side of the massive wolf's head onto his coat, but Becca couldn't tell if the blood was hers or his, and honestly at that moment she didn't care. All she knew was that the wolf had finally released her leg and retreated over to his fallen mate giving Becca time to pick up her badly injured pet and carry her back to the cabin. She winced with every step she took. Her foot could barely take her own weight, much less the additional thirty-five pound dog, but she realized if she hesitated, the wolf would likely attack again, and she would surely lose the next battle.

As she climbed the porch steps, she took a moment to look back. The female wolf was beginning to stir as the male continued to lick the blood from her face. Becca could tell that she had done some real damage to the wolf, and was sorry that it had to happen. Sensing her staring at him, the male wolf turned those icy blue eyes toward Becca. There was no missing the look of pure hatred she saw in that piercing glare, and her blood instantly turned to ice. There was no doubt in her mind that if given the opportunity, the big male would certainly kill her. Anxious to get somewhere safe, she edged open the screen door and carried the whimpering dog inside.

Laying Sadie gently down on the kitchen table, Becca hurried into the bunk room and removed the first aid kit from the storage chest. Working quickly, she filled a pot with water from the pump and put it on the fire to heat. Returning to her pet, she stroked the soft fur and whispered soothingly to her until Sadie stopped trembling. Wiping the tears from her cheeks, Becca poured some of the now heated water into the dishpan and grabbing a clean cloth, began to wash away the blood. There were lots of wounds all over Sadie's body, but most were nothing more than shallow scratches, with the exception of the initial bite to her shoulder. It was deep and ugly. Raw skin was visible through the blood, but it didn't appear to have gone as deep as the bone. Gently cleaning the wound with the warm water and then with antiseptic, she closed the torn skin with several butterfly bandages as well as she could. Taking a pressure bandage from the kit, she carefully lifted Sadie's upper body and wrapped it tightly around her to hold the gauze in place. The gentle lab looked up at her with pain-wracked eyes and Becca began to cry again. She blamed herself for putting the dog in danger by taking her outside. How stupid she had been! She should have been more careful, but how could she have known what would happen?

Brushing away the tears with the backs of her hands, she took two aspirin out of the kit and crushed them with a spoon. Then mixing the powder with some of the peanut butter, she let Sadie lick it off. Hopefully, it would help to stem any infection, but at the very least, it might ease the dog's pain a bit. Sadie's breathing was becoming regular again and she had stopped the pitiful mewling, so Becca gently lifted her up and carried her into the bunk room. Placing her on one of the empty beds and covering her with a blanket in case she went into shock, she returned to the kitchen to take care of her own injury.

She knew nothing had been broken, because she could still walk, but removing the ruined boot brought about a whole new wave of pain. Blood from the wound had pooled inside her boot. Once she had wiped the blood away with the warm, soapy water, she was horrified to see just how bad the damage was. White bone could be clearly seen in a couple of the larger gashes.

"This is going to need a few stitches, I think," she said miserably. Having barely passed sewing in her home economics class, Becca shook her head ruefully. Could she do it herself? Surely someone would be coming for her soon and then she and Sadie could get medical care from people who actually knew what they're doing! No, she knew she couldn't wait because she had absolutely no idea how long it would be before help arrived.

Reaching back inside the first aid kit, she took out the needle and thread that she found there. Wishing she had a good stiff shot of alcohol, even though she really didn't like to drink, Becca braced herself for what she knew was coming. Even being as mentally prepared as she could be, the agony she felt from the very first puncture of the needle was incredible. She bit down hard on her lip and with shaking hands continued inserting and drawing out the needle and thread until the larger holes were closed nearly passing out from the pain. Twice she had to pause because she felt lightheaded, but she managed to finish. Then she doused all of the wounds she had suffered with hydrogen peroxide, applied a generous amount of the antibiotic ointment onto the wound, and gingerly wrapped her ankle in gauze and clean bandages. For good measure, she swallowed four of the aspirin dry.

Now that the initial adrenalin rush was over, just like a balloon losing air, Becca found she was exhausted. Thinking about how much damage she and Sadie had suffered from the unprovoked wolf attacks, and yet knowing it could have been so much worse, Becca began sobbing - both from relief and residual fear. She knew they were safe from the wolves for now, but still a long, long way from home. She had never felt so completely alone in her whole life. Laying her head down onto her arms, she cried until she finally fell asleep.

Chapter Fifteen

January 9th

Trooper Sammy Dix got the call from the radio dispatcher about four o'clock to go to the emergency cabin on highway 149 and pick up a stranded driver. After all of the problems the highway patrol had had to deal with the over the past few days, he was delighted to have been tapped for this mundane task. It offered him a chance to decompress a little. Whenever the weather worked against them, and the inevitable snarls and car crashes occurred, tensions ran high. Sammy was just coming off a long double shift, and as soon as he had delivered this particular package to wherever they needed to go, he would be heading straight home to tall bourbon and a soft, warm bed.

His wife, Rachelle, had left him two years ago, because she said she couldn't take not knowing when, or sometimes if, he would be coming home at night. He later found out that her apparent anxiety wasn't due to any real concern for his overall safety as she had insisted for years, but more out of concern that he might show up unexpectedly while she was entertaining one of her other men. She had wound up marrying one of her lovers from that period only one month after their divorce was final. Sammy hadn't been sorry to see her go and he hadn't contested the proceedings. Rachelle got her divorce and Sammy got everything else. The house, the SUV, even the dog! She didn't want anything that they had bought together during their six year marriage and that was fine with him! Tonight he was really looking forward to being able to stretch out on the king-size bed and watching a little ESPN. Something that he would never have been able to do if Rachelle had still been around.

The sound of a powerful car engine woke Becca from her sleep. Her neck was stiff and her back sore from the way she had slept, but she rose to see where the noise was coming from. It wasn't until she looked out of the front window and saw the Highway Patrol vehicle slowly and very carefully negotiating along the track to the cabin that she realized the help she had been praying for was finally coming. Smiling broadly, she began to rush around the cabin gathering her personal items together so that she'd be ready as soon as the trooper managed to get there. Looking down she was surprised when she realized that she was still wearing the tee shirt with Sadie's blood across the front. Instantly, the shock and horror that had transpired earlier came rushing back. Moving into the bunk room, she first checked on her dog, happy to find her still sleeping peacefully. Then she hastily removed the bloody shirt and pulled on an old worn SMU sweatshirt from days gone by. Anxious to get out of the nightmare she had had to endure for days, she continued collecting those items she would be taking with her and stuffing them into her carryall.

Trooper Dix pulled the 4-wheel drive SUV as close as possible to the cabin, but the snow drifts prevented him from getting closer than twenty-five feet or so. "Well, looks like this is the best I can do," he thought. "They'll just have to hoof it to here."

Opening the door of his cruiser, Sammy got out of the car and sank up to his knees in the wet snow. Stretching his back broadly, he adjusted his belt and managed to drop his car keys. He bent down pick them up and when he rose, he was shocked to see two wolves standing no more than ten feet in front of the car. Where had they come from? He hadn't heard a thing! Sammy had seen wolves before while driving through the national forest, but they typically avoided contact with humans and he had never given them much thought. He had certainly never been this close to one and he wasn't exactly sure what he should do. A movement off to his left suddenly captured his attention, and when he turned to look, he was horrified to see two additional wolves moving out from the shadowy tree line towards him. The obvious alpha male was massive through the chest area and Sammy estimated its weight at close to a hundred and eighty pounds. While the trooper stared open-mouthed, the silver wolf's mouth pulled back to reveal a set of sharp, white teeth. To Sammy, each canine looked to be 3 inches long. A throaty growl came from deep in the wolf's chest and saliva dripped from its fangs.

Sammy slowly slid his hand over to release the strap securing his service pistol on his hip, but immediately froze when the big gray wolf began its slow approach. The wolf was easily larger than his sister's 165 pound mastiff and the man could tell there was real power behind the way the muscles moved beneath his fur. The alpha kept his silver-blue eyes focused intently on the man standing in front of him and he could smell the fear coming off of him in waves. Risking a quick look back toward the first two wolves he had seen, Sammy was surprised to find that they had also been moving closer towards him and now stood only a couple of feet away from the SUVs front bumper. With the car door open, he realized that it offered a little protection from the wolves advancing from the front of the automobile, but he was completely vulnerable to the alpha male approaching from the side.

Beginning to feel the panic building within, he desperately grabbed hold of his pistol. He had barely gotten it free of the holster when the huge grey wolf jumped him, clamping down hard on the wrist holding the gun with his teeth. The trooper felt the wolf's incisors sink deep into his flesh and cried out when the sharp canines started to grind against the bone. That was when he heard and felt the terrible crack of his wrist breaking. Screaming from the sudden pain of his ravaged wrist, he dropped both the pistol and the car keys to the snowy ground. Sammy used his free hand to desperately try to pry the jaws of the wolf from his now useless hand. The alpha wolf suddenly released the terrified trooper's wrist and, instead, leapt up to bite deeply into the man's shoulder. With an incredible show of strength, the big gray wolf viciously pulled the flailing trooper away from the SUV releasing him. A second after he hit the ground, Sammy felt more teeth bite into his calf as one of the wolves that had been at the front of the vehicle brutally attacked his leg.

In full panic now and wracked with more pain than he thought imaginable, Sammy Dix clung to the hope that if he could just break free long enough to get back into the safety of his car, he would be alright. Clawing desperately at the upholstery with all the strength he could muster, he kicked out to free himself from the wolf that was currently chewing on his leg and pulled himself slowly into the SUV. Unfortunately, as he grabbed hold of the steering wheel to help him crawl across the driver's seat, a third wolf leapt onto his back, knocking the wind out of his lungs and biting off the fingers of his left hand like they were twigs. Crying out for help, the desperate trooper tried to roll over, but the steering wheel only let him make it halfway round leaving him completely vulnerable to attack. The man felt his bladder release as he came nearly nose to nose with the horror standing above him in the doorway with its jaws wide open, and Sammy screamed in terror. The alpha wolf was massive in size and heavy with muscle, its body crushing Sammy's chest under its weight. The man's eyes widened with fear when the wolf leaned in closer and he could feel the hot, fetid breath wash over his skin. The wolf momentarily paused as it looked down on its victim as if waiting for the man to do something, but Sammy's mind had completely broken. Then there was nothing, but teeth and flying saliva as it opened its huge maw and ripped into the soft flesh at the trooper's exposed throat. Sammy stopped struggling as a geyser of rich, red blood erupted from the wound and painted the inside windows crimson. He was dead within seconds.

Becca carried her bag in from the bunk room and set it down on the table. As she was returning to get Sadie and carry her into the main room, she heard a strange noise and stopped to glance out the front window. Looking out, she wasn't surprised to see that snow was falling once again, but something struck her as odd about the scene. She couldn't immediately tell what it was that bothered her. Then it hit her. The Highway Patrol vehicle was parked a little way up the drive, and the door was standing open, but she didn't see the driver anywhere. Had he walked up to the cabin? She turned to look both ways on the porch, but could see nothing.

Suddenly, a strangled cry was heard coming from the direction of the cruiser causing her head to snap back. From the angle of the window along with the continuously shifting shadows being caused by the increasing winds and nearby trees, she had a difficult time focusing in on what was actually happening, but she could see that a lot of movement was taking place inside the vehicle itself. Making matters worse, at that moment, something seemed to explode across the windshield, making it nearly impossible for her to determine exactly what was happening.

Squinting into the shifting light and shadows, she was finally able to focus on the car itself and with a gasp, realized that what was obscuring the window was not dirt, but blood - lots and lots of blood. "On my God! No, no, no, NO!" she screamed aloud.

There was so much blood that it not only covered the glass in a viscous curtain of gore, but also ran out of the open door and had begun pooling on the pristine white snow that lay on the ground outside the car, even as fresh snow continued to fall. It was like something from out Dante's vision of Hell.

As Becca watched in abject horror, she saw an extremely large wolf begin to back away from the open door, savagely pulling a limp body out of the car with it. A second wolf began ripping into the leg of the ravaged trooper and was rewarded with a piece of bloody meat. Even through her shock, Becca's brain registered that she hadn't seen any movement of the trooper's leg while the wolf was removing pieces of flesh and that most likely meant he was already dead. Undeniably, the sheer amount of blood loss would have been enough to kill him.

Becca stifled a second scream with her fist as she watched the wolves jumping in and out of the car; their bodies literally slavered in blood and gore as they ripped the clothing and flesh from the dead trooper with equal ferocity. Thankfully, the angle of the SUV to the window of the cabin prevented her from seeing the worst of the carnage, but enough was visible to fill her nightmares for weeks to come. Finally sated, the big silver male walked away from the body. He took a few steps in the direction of the cabin, his steely blue eyes never leaving Becca's as if daring her to come outside. Then he sat down in the deepening drifts and began to lick the mess of bloody tissue and sinew from its fur. As horrible as it was, she found that she couldn't turn away from the tableau. Fighting back the burning taste of bile that rose in her throat, she continued to stare out the window as she backed away from the gruesome display. It was as if she thought by doing so, she could deny what was happening, but the nightmare continued.

Now that she was far enough away from the window so she no longer had to witness the brutal attack taking place right in front of her, Becca felt possessed by the terror that continued to escalate inside of her. What could she do? How was she going to make it out of here now? Ben's deep voice instantly came to mind, and she rushed to the phone. With trembling fingers, she picked up the receiver and pushed the emergency button. It rang once and then was picked up on the other end. Her knees nearly buckled when she heard the familiar masculine voice.

"Hi, Becca," he greeted her warmly. "What's up?"

Becca swallowed hard, and through a fresh veil of tears managed to choke out "Oh, my God, Ben! He's dead! They've killed him. Oh, my God! It's so horrible!"

Ben was confused by what she was screaming, but there was no mistaking the panic in her voice, and so he asked her to explain. She was barely coherent as she tried to explain the grizzly scene still taking place outside the cabin.

The ranger listened in disbelief, but remained silent while she spoke. All he wanted to do was to take her in his arms and comfort her. This was someone he had never actually met in person, and yet his need to protect her was palpable. When she had run out of breath and dissolved into tears, Ben finally responded.

"Are you alright, Becca? You and Sadie?" he asked softly, genuine concern in his voice.

Realizing with a shock, that he didn't know about the earlier attack on Sadie and herself, she confessed, "No, we are definitely not okay! The wolves also attacked Sadie and me earlier today."

"What! When? What happened?" Ben questioned. "Tell me exactly what happened!"

Becca recited the episode from the time the pair had first gone outside, to Sadie's provocative behavior toward the big gray, to the attack of the she-wolf and finally how the male had assaulted her. The longer she talked, the more her speech became colorless. Ben was struck by her detached description of the savage attack she had suffered, and he quickly recognized the signs of shock. He knew from the dull, somnambulant way she was talking that she would only continue to sink into a deeper depression, unless he could stop it. There was no emotion in her words, no life, only an extreme weariness. He had witnessed PTSD first hand while in the Afghanistan, and he knew how devastating it could be. Some people he knew had never recovered. His heart ached for this young woman, and he was determined to save her. Pulling himself up, he recognized that his first priority was to pull her back to the present.

"Well, it sounds like you've had quite a day!" he quipped with humor he in no way felt.

The thoughtless comment after all of the stark brutality she had just witnessed filled her with an instant fury, and she reacted immediately.

"You heartless, insensitive son of a bitch! How dare you act so callous! There's a man I never even had a chance to meet lying out there in the snow being ripped to shreds by those beasts you told me wouldn't bother us and yet I've been attacked, my dog was nearly killed and a man is dead because of them! I never would have believed that you could be so unfeeling, cold-blooded and cruel if I hadn't heard it for myself". Taking a ragged breath, she continued, "You sit in your treetop tower of power like some damn pompous forest overlord never taking responsibility for anything, and when someone else actually steps up to help, and winds up a bloody corpse, I might add, all you can say is "well, you've had a bad day". Well, screw you, Ranger Ben. Go back to cataloging your squirrels and chipmunks or whatever it is you actually do. The rest of us will somehow manage to survive without you. Or, maybe we won't, but we won't be looking to you for help."

He felt as if she had just stabbed him in the heart. The venomous way she spit out her words had caught him by total surprise, but he was gratified that his ruse had forced such a visceral reaction from her. Now he had to tread lightly and bring her back down. Speaking like he would have to an injured animal, Ben began by apologizing.

"I'm so sorry, Becca, if I seemed uncaring, because that is far from the case. The fact is, I was good friends with Sammy, uh, Trooper Dix. We've known each other since high school and have spent a lot of time backpacking and hunting together. I was best man at his wedding and supported him through his divorce. What happened to him today is a guilt that I will have to live with for the rest of my life. You see, I was the one who requested as a favor to me that he personally pick you up and take you on to your ranch," he continued, "When we received word from the weather bureau that the backside of the front would hit later today and would undoubtedly be worse than what we experienced so far, I wanted to get you out of there quickly. I can only imagine how horrible this entire day has to have been for you, and yes, I have some guilt to deal with in that regard, too, because you're right. I did tell you that you would be safe, and you obviously aren't. Even without Sadie's being in season, I didn't believe that the wolves were a real threat and so I sat here in my, how did you describe it? My "treetop tower of power," and I got to talk with a strong, intelligent, funny lady who was determined to take a bad situation and make the best of it. I was understandably impressed, and I still am, but after being in combat and seeing strong men fall to PTSD, I feared that what I was hearing in your voice was the same thing. I had to bring you back from the brink before you gave up entirely for your sake, and for Sadie's. If that happened, you would never survive. The only way I could think of to do that was to get you riled up. So, I made that callous remark." He paused before adding, "I hope that you will forgive me, but I will certainly understand if you can't."

The overwhelming sadness in his voice over the loss of his friend spoke volumes directly to

Becca's heart and she wished she could reach out and hold him in her arms. Instead, choking on the gambit of emotions she felt, she managed to say, "I forgive you, Ben, and I sincerely apologize for my hateful tirade. I let my Irish temper take hold and you just got hit with both barrels."

With a hollow laugh, Ben said, "You don't need to apologize for anything, but now we need to figure out the fastest way to get you away from there."

Chapter Sixteen

As the alpha male remained by the car solemnly watching the building for the woman or the dog, Notch-Ear and the two females dragged the bloody remains of Trooper Dix deeper into the shadow of the woods toward the wolf's den. They would all need to feed again soon, and there was still meat and marrow to be had by all. The blood on the body was already beginning to crystalize from the freezing temperature, but it wouldn't deter the wolves from feasting on the corpse again at their leisure. The carcass left an obvious trail, but the grisly tracks were quickly being filled in by the pure white falling snow. Soon, the only indication that anything unusual had taken place would be the abandoned patrol car.

In the meantime, the alpha male patiently watched and waited.

* * * * * * * *

Pacing back and forth as far as the phone cord would allow, Becca listened carefully to what Ben was saying.

"The first thing I've got to do is notify the highway patrol about what's happened to Sammy. I'm sure that they will want to send a crew out to retrieve the body. You should be able to get a ride out with them."

"But what about the wolves?" Becca asked. "They might still be out there. I couldn't live with myself if any more people were hurt or, God forbid, killed because of them."

Nodding, Ben agreed. "You're right. We definitely don't want to put more lives in danger, but at least they will come prepared. Can you please take a quick look outside just to see if they're still in the vicinity of the cabin?"

She didn't want to go anywhere near the window, much less look at the bloody carnage outside, but Becca understood that there was no other option. Approaching the glass reluctantly, she was completely dumbstruck by what she saw.

"Ben, the only wolf still there is the big male," she said softly.

"That's good! He'll probably follow the rest back into the woods."

"Maybe," she said doubtfully. Swallowing, she continued, "but, Ben? The body isn't there anymore."

The silence from the other end of the line lingered for several seconds before the young ranger asked, "What are you talking about, Becca? Where is the body?"

Becca was shaking her head in puzzlement and she stammered, "I .. I don't know. There isn't anything left out there! In fact, I can hardly tell where the attack occurred ... and I watched whole thing!"

Her voice continued to rise in pitch as she continued, "If the car weren't still there, I would think I imagined it all, but the inside of the windshield is still covered in blood and icicles of blood are dripping from the car door, so I know for sure that the nightmare happened. It's just that the snow has covered all of the blood that had been on the ground, and Sammy's body is gone! It's completely gone, Ben! What could have happened to it?"

A chill ran through his body as he answered, "Obviously, the wolves must have drug the body off somewhere. Probably so they can continue to feed off it later," Ben responded hollowly. In his mind he was picturing his friend's body being mauled again and again by the wolves, and it sickened him. All he wanted to do was grab his rifle and ... no, he had to stop thinking like that right now. His first priority was to calm Becca down and decide the best way to get her out of there safely.

All of a sudden, a loud howl came from the bunk room. Ben heard it and asked, "What's that noise?"

"It's Sadie!" Becca replied, the surprise obvious in her voice. "What is she doing?"

Dropping the handset to the floor where it clattered against the hardwood floor and was pulled back to the wall by the cord. She raced into the adjoining bunk room to find Sadie standing at the window by her bed and whining piteously. Becca moved to the window and realized that Sadie had a clear view of the huge grey wolf. Worse yet, she realized that the wolf was staring directly at the window. Looking at her pet in dismay, she was shocked to realize that she wanted to go outside! To him! Becca was furious! Here was her dog, her best friend and companion, whining to get to the monster that had not only attacked her mistress, but also viciously killed an innocent man! Abruptly, Becca stopped and realized how ridiculous she was being. Sadie couldn't fight her natural instinct to mate any more than she could stop breathing. In an effort to calm Sadie down, she pulled the window shade all the way down effectively cutting the male wolf from Sadie's view.

She sat on the bed and rubbed the dog's soft black fur for several seconds and spoke to her soothingly. Then Becca ran back to the phone and sobbing, said, "Oh, Ben, what am I going to do? Sadie is trying to get out to him. I'm so scared he's going to get in."

Compartmentalizing his sadness over the loss of his friend to deal with privately at a later time, the ranger drew once again on his professional training. "Don't worry. Just stay in the cabin and make sure all of the doors are securely bolted. He won't be able to get in the cabin and Sadie won't get out. I am going to go ahead and notify the authorities about Sammy, but since there is not body to collect, I doubt that they will make it a priority to send anyone else out, especially with the new storm front moving through bringing a whole new mess of problems that they will have to deal with." Pausing, he added, "In fact, I will insist that they <u>don't</u> do that for the present since we aren't sure where all the wolves are at this point."

Nodding her head vigorously, Becca responded with "Okay. I understand what you're saying, and I know that I really have no choice, but to trust that you know the best thing to do. I do, Ben. I trust you."

Accepting the weight of this added responsibility sitting heavily on his shoulders, Ben went on. "Look. It's going to be dark soon and the bad weather is moving in already, so nothing is going to happen tonight. I just need for you to stay strong for a few more hours. Then, in the morning, I'll come for you myself. I swear it."

Becca nearly collapsed with the sense of relief his promise provided, but just as quickly as it had come, concern now blossomed. "But then you'll be in danger from the wolves, won't you?"

"I will, but believe me. I'll come prepared and they won't take me by surprise like they did Sammy," he responded. He couldn't deny the joy he felt at being the subject of her obvious concern. "I just need for you to hang in there for a little while longer. Can you do that for me?"

"Sure," she answered without conviction. "I'm sure we'll be fine till I see you tomorrow." Then, with a nervous laugh she added, "Just don't be late! We're counting on you!"

"Not a chance. I'll be there as soon as I can, and remember," he cautioned. "If you get scared or anything happens tonight, just pick up the phone. I'm here for you, Becca."

Smiling with joy at how that simple statement could make her feel, she said, "I know, Ben, and you can't know how much that has meant to me. Seriously, that's really the only thing keeping me from shaving my head and sitting cross legged in the middle of the living room chanting there's no place like home right now. Maybe when this is all over, we could get together and share a bottle of wine."

"My treat," Ben replied with a smile. He couldn't help, but grin at her attempt to find humor in a horrible situation. "Heck, I'll even spring for dinner at Barney's Grille!" Becca could hear him smiling through the phone line and for the first time in what seemed like a very long time, she felt excited by the possibility of meeting this man face-to-face. She actually found herself looking forward to the prospect as they both said goodbye and she hung up the phone.

Chapter Seventeen

Sadie trotted into the main room of the cabin and went directly up to Becca. She was sensing her mistress's anxiety, so she sat down in front of her and laying her big black head on her knees. Sadie turned those brown soulful eyes up to look at Becca as if to ask "what do we do now?" Becca gently stroked the soft fur along the lab's neck and lovingly told her, "It's going to be alright, girl. Just one more night, that's all and then Ben's coming for us and we'll get out of here finally."

Suddenly realizing with everything that had been happening, neither she nor her dog had eaten anything since breakfast, and after all that she had witnessed today, she was surprised at just how hungry she actually was. Looking back down at Sadie, she asked, "Are you hungry, girl?" which instantly garnered the dog's "happy dance," her nails tapping musically across the wood floor.

Standing up, she said out loud to break the quiet, "Okay, girl, let's check out Old Mother

Hubbard's cupboard, and see what we can find."

Lifting the cover of the storage chest, Becca selected two packages of the freeze dried spaghetti in a meat sauce. Stoking up the embers in the fireplace, she added another log on top. Taking the big aluminum pot from the hook, she went and filled it with water from the pump, then returned it to hang directly over the flames now licking around the edges of the wood. Taking down two plates and cutlery for one, she then carried the bread and peanut butter to the table.

"How about an appetizer before dinner?"

The long, sleek tail of the lab beat a staccato rhythm in anticipation of one of her favorite treats. Becca first crushed another aspirin and mixed it with the peanut butter she spread on half a piece of bread. She was leaning over to present the tasty snack to Sadie, when the dog surprised her by rising up suddenly and snatching the bread from her hand. Becca barely had time to pull back.

"Okay, I get it," Becca said. "You're hungry. Well, so am I. Let me get this party started."

Walking back to the now boiling pot of water, she carried it over the kitchen counter. Pouring most of the water into the dishpan for later use, she added the contents of the packaged food to the remaining water and stirred. Soon the room was filled with the rich, heady aroma of tomato sauce and made Becca's stomach growl loudly. Once the meal had been mixed together, the pasta becoming limp and the sauce started to thicken nicely, Becca could wait no longer. She spooned up a large amount of the food onto the two plates and carried them to the table. Returning to the pump, she quickly filled both a glass and Sadie's water bowl with the icy spring water. She had to laugh that might as she set the bowl down on the floor, because she noticed that not only had Sadie not moved since Becca had placed the steaming plates on the tabletop, she had also not taken her eyes off them as if she worried disappear. Walking over and sitting down at the table, Becca took one of the plates and set it down on the floor. Sadie immediately took over and in less than two minutes had licked the plate clean.

Not really expecting any response from the dog, she teased, "Good Lord, Sadie! Did you even chew it or just swallowed it whole?"

She tore a piece of bread and as she started to dip it into the rich red sauce on her plate, the image of the bloodied body of Trooper Dix returned in an instant and Becca had to rush to the chemical toilet to be sick. Sitting back and closing her eyes, she tried to calm down. When she got up and returned to the kitchen, she wasn't surprised to find Sadie sitting in front of her watching her intently. Becca smiled, happy to see that the dog hadn't apparently lost her appetite after today's trials. Knowing that there was no way she herself would be able to eat the spaghetti, she picked up her untouched plate and placed it on the floor to the obvious delight of the pup.

Picking up a knife, she began spreading peanut butter on a piece of dry bread when she was distracted by an odd sound. Though Sadie seemed to recognize it immediately for what it was, it took Becca a few seconds to understand that it was the sound of the big, gray wolf trying to scratch his way in through the screen door. Becca heard a metallic ripping and understood that he has successfully torn through the thin mesh. Now he was clawing feverously at the thick wooden door. His grunting seemed to get louder as he became more and more frustrated by his efforts. Sadie paced back and forth in front of the door with an occasional glance back at Becca, whining. Whether the dog was unhappy that her mistress wouldn't let him in, or because she was afraid that she actually would, Becca only sat rigidly at the table.

"He can't get in. He can't get in," she kept repeating the mantra to herself. Over the next ten minutes, the frenetic scratching and growling sounds slowed down until they finally ceased completely. Now that the excitement was over, Sadie walked over and lay down on the rug in front of the fire as if nothing had happened, and Becca visibly relaxed. From the dog's actions, she knew that the wolf must have left, but just to be sure, she got up and walked over to look out of the front window. Movement to the right caught her eye and she turned just in time to see the beast disappear into the tree line like a ghost. Snow continued to fall heavily and her visibility deteriorated. She no longer saw any sign of the wolf. Returning to table, she finished eating her dinner of peanut butter and bread.

Nothing else happened during her meal, so she picked up the dirty dishes and dropped them into the waiting dishpan. Adding soap, she carefully washed and rinsed them, laying them on paper towels placed on the counter to dry. Craving something more, she refilled the pot with water and placed it over the fire for hot chocolate. Then she returned to the counter to finish washing the dishes. Reaching over, Becca opened the small café window that was set high on the wall next to the counter. It wasn't very large at all. Maybe only eighteen inches square, but without a drain in the "sink" and not wanting to risk going outside, she had to get rid of the dirty dishwater somehow. So, she picked up the dishpan of dirty water and threw it out of the window. Instantly a large silver-gray face with piercing blue eyes and a mouth flashing curved sharp teeth leapt up towards the open window, snarling and snapping with its best efforts to reach her. The massive front paws momentarily extended over the window frame and she could hear scratching against the wall as the wolf tried to climb up the side of the cabin. Becca gasped at the razor-sharp claws that extended over the sill, but then the wolf fell back out of sight. Totally taken by surprise by the encounter, she had dropped the nearly empty plastic container and gasped loudly. She could hear the wolf as it continued to growl and scratch at the wall below the window, but he didn't attempt to reach the window again. Shaking uncontrollably and keeping out of sight, she warily walked to the side of the window and closed it as quietly as possible. After engaging the lock, she turned her back, closed her eyes, and leaned heavily against the solid wall thankful to have such a strong barricade between her and the hateful beast. With her heart still racing with fright and salty tears rolling down her cheeks, she slid down the wall until she was sitting on the plank floor, her knees tucked up under her chin. There she remained for several minutes until her heart resumed its normal rhythm.

"Oh, Ben, please hurry," she whispered softly to herself. "I don't know how much longer I can do this."

Chapter Eighteen

The ranger knew that there was nothing he could immediately do to help Becca, and he found that he couldn't relax. Night was falling fast and he needed a plan. He was too invested in this young woman whom he had yet to meet in person to think about anything else. Ben was surprised to realize just how much he cared about her and knowing that she was essentially alone and trapped out there with those vicious animals caused him to pace restlessly around the station. Walking into the kitchen area for the third time in the last half hour, he refilled his cup with hot coffee and decided to work on whatever options might be available to him. His five year old trailblazer was parked at the railhead over half a mile away, but even with its 4-wheel drive, he knew he wouldn't make it on the highway and it would be virtually useless over the incredibly rough and uneven terrain that he would need to cover in the treacherous weather. That left him with only one other resource.

Pulling on his anorak, insulated knit cap and thermal gloves, he left the warmth and shelter of the building and trudged through the deepening drifts until he reached the doors of the double-wide utility shed sitting nearby. Glistening slivers of ice began to collect quickly on his eyebrows and in his beard. Unlocking the large clasp that held the extra-large doors closed against the strong wind gusts, he had a hard time sliding the barn doors wide enough for him to enter. Once inside, the gloomy interior was like something out of a Hawthorne novel. The wind whistled around the windows, but couldn't get in. Shadows filled the corners and worked to obscure the items housed there. The below freezing temperatures caused his lungs to burn when he inhaled and his breath to hang in the still air like white spider webs. Rubbing his gloved hands together, he reached over and turned on the overhead fluorescent light. It buzzed, but Ben found the bright light reassuring. Turning, he walked purposefully toward a large mound that rose from the rear of the building and was covered by a brown canvas tarp.

Jerking the heavy canvas cover off, he revealed the shiny red Alpena Sherpa ATSS snowmobile. The machine had high peak torque and a 75 horse powered engine. It would easily be able to handle the trip to the cabin without any issues. Unlike the usual snowmobiles enjoyed by winter sports enthusiasts everywhere, this one had been specifically modified by the manufacturer for use by the forestry service. The chassis was built a full 6 inches higher than normal to raise it above the rocky terrain and the dual wide track skis could handle the deepest snow with ease. As with all snowmobiles, the driver's console and seat were not enclosed. The driver and one passenger could straddle the leather seat very comfortably, but what made it so unique was that when additional seating was necessary, a small bench had been added by the manufacturer. This bench could be fitted onto the rear allowing room for an additional four men. This extra seating had proven handy in the past when teams needed to be shuttled back and forth to fight forest fires. In addition, when times called for extra storage space, the bench could be easily removed to reveal an open three by four foot area. Twelve inch tall metal rails could also be installed to convert the space from passenger seating to carrying emergency equipment safely and securely. Currently, the bench hid a fenced-in area that was filled with a couple of chainsaws, a drum of fire retardant chemicals, an axe, a toolbox, three solar blankets and a well-stocked first aid kit.

Ben removed everything from the snow cat, except for the blankets and the first aid kit. This would allow enough room for Sadie to lie down while the machine was in motion. To the left of the snow cat, sat a second, smaller canvas-covered mound. With a flourish, Ben pulled off the cover and exposed the Moose cargo sled. Maneuvering the bulky piece of equipment took some time, but he eventually got it into the right position and attached it to the snowmobile. This accessory came with a retractable cover and would provide more than enough space for whatever baggage Becca needed to take with her from the cabin. It would also come in handy should he come across Sammy's remains. Lastly, he checked to make sure that the engine's tank was filled with gas. As an afterthought, he filled a five-gallon can with extra fuel and strapped it onto the sled.

Working steadily and physically pushing himself in the freezing temperatures helped to release some of the tension from his body, but not in his mind. He couldn't stop thinking about the very real danger that they were all going to be in during the extraction. The wolf pack now had a taste for human blood and they obviously no longer had any fear of man. They also wouldn't be hesitant about attacking the sled and anyone riding on it. The open air vehicle would provide absolutely no protection from either the elements or the wolves, so he knew he needed to come up with a way to improve their chances of survival.

Leaving the storage shed, he returned to the warmth of the ranger station and went directly to the locked weapons closet. From inside, he withdrew a Mossberg 30-06, a Smith and Wesson pistol, and a package of emergency road flares. Grabbing a box of extra ammunition and a rifle scabbard, he walked back through the heavily falling wet snow to the storage shed. After loading the rifle with bullets, he affixed the scabbard to the side of the console with duct tape so that the rifle could easily be extracted when needed. The package of flares and the box of spare ammunition he dropped into the open storage compartment built into the console of the cat. The pistol he would keep on his belt along with his ten inch Buck knife. He realized that these two items would likely be used as a last resort, but he felt better just having them handy.

Deciding at last that he was as prepared as he could possibly be, he recovered the snowmobile with the tarp to keep it protected from the dropping temperature, closed the shed door and returned to the station. Although his body was exhausted, he felt certain that he would never be able to find sleep this night. Too many details and worries continued to circulate through his thoughts. Ben shrugged out of his heavy outer clothing shaking the snow and ice off, leaving it to melt in a pool by the door. Blowing on his frozen hands as he crossed the room, he walked to the large window and stood watching the falling snow. It continued to fall carpeting everything like wet cotton. He knew it wouldn't be long before his tracks to the shed would disappear under the continuing snowfall. Turning back, he sat down in a well-worn leather chair in front of the Franklin stove and absently picked up his now cold coffee. After taking a sip of the unappealing brew, Ben untied his wet boots and set them aside to dry. Then, he raised his stockinged feet up on the wood box where he could relish in the heat from the stove. Sinking back into the depths of the chair, Ben closed his eyes and turned his thoughts to Becca. He had ever known a woman who had shown the core strength that she had during this whole mess. He couldn't think of a man either, for that matter. Sure, she was scared, but who wouldn't be. The brutal attack on his friend had happened right in front of her, but she hadn't panicked. Instinctively, she seemed to realize that if she and Sadie were going to make it through this ordeal, she had to stay focused and be ready to do whatever she could to ensure their survival.

Ben found himself looking forward to finally meeting the mystery woman from the other end of the line. Keeping his eyes closed, he started trying to form a mental picture of what Becca Thornton might look like, but then decided that it really didn't matter. All he knew was that she intrigued him in a way no other woman ever had. It was her spunk, toughness, and courage that attracted him to her like a kid to candy. Looks had always been secondary to him when dating. He found he was more interested in those women who showed intelligence, confidence and self-assurance, rather than the ones overly concerned with their make-up, hairstyles, and the current fashion trends. Becca has those qualities in spades. He wanted to find a companion with like interests, not some hot house flower needing constant affirmation of their small, unimportant accomplishments.

Slowly, the heat from the fire and his physical exhaustion began to work on the ranger, and as he began to drift off, his last thoughts were actually a promise to himself that he was going to do whatever it took for him to reach and save Rebecca Thornton. Tomorrow she would no longer by a fantasy to him, but the real thing.

Chapter Nineteen
January 10th

The next morning arrived with the sun slicing through the gray scattered clouds in buttery colored slivers. A light powdery snow was falling and it sparkled like diamond crystals wherever the sun hit it, but deeper in the shadows hiding in among the trees, the snowdrifts were deep. There had been no further incidents during the night, and Becca reluctantly awoke from a very special dream where she and ranger Ben had been picnicking near a crystal blue lake on a beautiful spring day. She couldn't actually see his face because his head was turned, but in the way of dreams, she knew it was him and that he was very handsome. They had made love in the grass and now they lay content and satisfied side by side. Becca felt the warm sun kiss her bare skin and sighed. Then the ranger turned towards her, his beautiful blue eyes locking onto hers and he leaned in for a kiss and …

A rough, wet tongue licked across her cheek causing her to sit straight up in the bed.

"Sadie!" she shrieked. Then seeing that the startled dog had jumped back, she leaned over laughing and put her arms around her sleek black neck. "Sorry, girl. You just surprised me out of a really nice dream!"

Putting her feet on the frigid floor, she looked at the bewildered dog and asked, "What's up, pup?"

That's when she smelled it. There was no mistaking the aroma of dog urine in the room. Sensing that her mistress would be angry upon discovering her biological faux pas, Sadie hung her head and whimpered apologetically. Smiling into those dark chocolate brown eyes, Becca soothed her by placing her forehead against the dog's and saying, "It's okay, Sadie. At least this time! I wouldn't have been able to take you outside anyway, so we'll just have to deal with it."

Brusquely rubbing Sadie's velvety head, Becca stood up and walked into the kitchen. Grabbing a handful of paper towels, she returned to find the dog still sitting where she had left her. As she wiped up Sadie's accident, a thought suddenly hit her. *Today is the day! We'll finally be getting out of this whole nightmare!* The sudden realization hit her like a splash of ice water in the face and her spirits began to soar.

Smiling happily, she began humming a Billy Joel song as she continued to clean up.

Sadie sensed her mistress's mood change and trotted happily after Becca as she took the now thoroughly soaked paper towels into the kitchen and threw them away. Becca was still humming to herself until she happened to look up at the window frame and cringed. The horror of the night before came crushing back. Immediately, her joyful frame of mind vanished and she moved very slowly toward the small aperture. Carefully looking out through the glass to make sure that the big wolf was nowhere in sight, she eased open the little window and wasn't surprised when she found the deep gouges that the wolf's sharp nails had carved into the wood. However, what had caught her eye was something much worse. There embedded in the wood was a claw of nearly three inches in length. Amazed by this discovery, Becca reached for the spur. It took some effort, but she finally pulled it out of the window sill and recognized blood on the end that would have been attached to the big wolf. She smiled with a mild sense of satisfaction as she carefully examined the deadly nail before dropping it on top of the wet paper towels in the nearby waste basket.

Staring down at it in amazement, Becca thought to herself, "So, it hadn't been a dream or hallucination." A shiver ran through her as she remembered how savage the wolf had been during his attempt to gain access to her and she quickly shut the window again. "It's okay," she murmured to the silent room. "He didn't get in, that's what matters, and Ben's coming today to get us, so everything will be okay." Taking a deep cleansing breath, she took a piece of dry paper towel and reached down, retrieving the frightening barb and laid it on top of the countertop. She would save the claw to show Ben when he arrived later that day.

Feeling a little bit better at the prospect of seeing the ranger, Becca went to the fireplace and after stirring up the embers, added a piece of wood to the pile. Before long, the fire was once again burning briskly. She knew logically that it wasn't likely Ben would be able to get there until mid-morning at the earliest, so she made a conscious effort to go about business as usual. Filling the cast iron pot with water, she placed it over the fire to heat and then headed into the bunk room to dress for the day. She felt it was important that she look nice when she met the ranger, so she chose a dark green angora sweater and black ski pants. She knew the green would make her own green eyes brighter and her pale skin to glow. Applying a touch of light makeup and taking out her hairbrush, she vigorously pulled it through her long mahogany-colored hair until it shined. At the last minute, she decided to add a spritz of J'Adore perfume. Couldn't hurt, right? After all, with sponge baths being the only option left to her over the past several days, she felt perfume was essential. Pleased with the overall effect, she began moving around the cabin straightening up. Finally she spent a few minutes collecting her things and putting them in her bag before returning to the main room.

By the time she had finished packing, the water was boiling. She moved about the room automatically, preparing the coffee to steep, refilling Sadie's water bowl and getting out a few packs of oatmeal. There were only a few pieces of bread left, and not wanting to have to carry it out once Ben arrived, she decided to spread peanut butter on all four slices. Becca poured herself some of the coffee and added the creamer and a healthy dose of sugar to it. She figured that she would need the extra energy today. Then mixing the oatmeal into the two bowls, she tore up two of the pieces of the peanut butter covered slices and dropped them into one of the bowls and set it down on the floor. Sadie wasted no time in cleaning her bowl, including licking up the few random drops of oatmeal off the floor that had escaped her initial attack.

Becca, in the meantime, sat down at the table and ate her meal automatically, but without any real interest. She was thinking back on the lovely dream she had been having when Sadie had abruptly awakened her and the anticipation of finally getting to meet the man from her dream. The memory of it made her blush as she sipped the hot coffee. More than just knowing she and Sadie would soon be out of the hell they had dealt with over the past few days, she was really looking forward to meeting her mystery man. His voice was so deep and sexy over the phone that Becca tingled at the very thought of it. She had never really had any serious relationships before, just a few dates now and then, but nothing ever came of them. Her primary focus had always been making junior partner at the law firm and having a serious boyfriend would only have been a distraction that would have gotten in the way of her ultimate goal. Becca wondered if this meeting could possibly lead to something really special for her. Could Ben turn out to be Mr. Right?

With those thrilling thoughts running through her mind, she had just started gathering up the dirty dishes when the howling began.

Chapter Twenty

The massive wolf lay concealed in the deep shadows within the forest, his attention riveted on the cabin only a hundred yards in front of him. The snow and ice crystals that clung to his thick grey fur blended so well with the color of his coat as to make him nearly invisible. He huffed out small white clouds of breath as he continually watched for any sign of movement from the cabin. This had been his focus for the past several hours ever since the female had thrown the water down on him. While the incident hadn't actually hurt him, it had definitely caught him by surprise. If he had only been able to reach her at that moment, he would have reveled in ripping her to pieces. However, the window had simply been too high. He could smell her fear in the air, though, and it had nearly driven him mad. In the process of trying to claw his way in, the wolf had lost a claw and the pain in his foot still throbbed painfully. Limping badly, he had paced along the perimeter of the building and finding no way in served to only build his frustration and rage. So intense was his focus on gaining access, that when his mate approached him and tried to offer him comfort, he viciously snapped back at her. Shocked by his sudden rebuke, she had tucked her tail between her legs and backed further into the trees. There she was joined by the two younger wolves. Since that time, the rest of the pack had left him alone, but still stayed near enough to be able to sense whatever he might do.

Shortly after dawn, Notch-Ear and the young female rose from the leaf litter and moved off deeper into the woods. Bewildered by their leader's preoccupation with the cabin, they had become bored. The entire pack had fed again during the night on what was left of the patrolman's remains, so hunger was not their immediate need. Instead, they felt the need to simply romp and play through the snow-laced brush and sun dappled forest.

The alpha female didn't follow the others, but lay just a few feet away from her mate and watched as he continuously licked his injured paw. After he had violently rejected her the night before, she had been careful to allow him his space. She was still very confused by his actions, but she could sense the tension in her mate and she remained silent. She was heavy with pups now and would likely be giving birth very soon. Her natural maternal instincts were telling her that she should be preparing her "nest," but she would not leave her mate.

When the sun was fully up, the big silver male stood and shook the winter crust from his fur. The she-wolf was immediately up and ready for whatever he was going to do, although she moved no closer to him. After taking a moment for a full body stretch, he turned away from the cabin and trotted a few feet away, his nose barley touching the snow pack. Eventually, he paused at the base of an aspen and relieved himself. Pungent steam from his hot urine stream rose thickly. Once he was done, he moved out of the shadows towards the lake with the female following closely behind. He stepped along the edge of the lake where the ice was thin until he heard a crack and water bubbled up from the newly created vent. Bending his head low over the partially frozen bank, he began to drink the frigid water. Standing a few feet away, the alpha female did the same until the female's body suddenly tensed causing the male to look sharply over at her. There was a strong odor coming off her, and he could see a string of bloody mucus hanging from her vulva. Her time to give birth had arrived.

Turning, she moved as quickly as could back through the forest to the pack's den with the alpha keeping pace beside her. Once inside the hollow, she moved around in a tight circular motion over the dirt and the dried vegetation until finally settling down next to the rock wall. Her breath was coming in short gasps now and her labor began in earnest. The male lay down nearby, but knew he wasn't needed and she wouldn't appreciate his interference in any case. The first pup arrived twenty minutes later. Deaf and blind at birth and weighing about the same as a can of coke, the tiny wolf immediately searched for his mother's teat and began nursing while she licked him clean. While the pup nursed, the she-wolf hungrily devoured the afterbirth to boost her energy level.

Two more cubs arrived over the next hour and were happily nursing while the satiated first pup slept next to the dam. The she-wolf was exhausted and snoring lightly, having expended a lot of energy during the births, but there had been no complications and all three pups were doing well. His curiosity getting the better of him, the alpha took the opportunity to move closer and sniff at the tiny new arrivals. He started to gently nudge the pups with his nose, causing them to lose their grip on the dam's nipples. Upset at being denied their mother's milk, the mewling cubs woke the female and she growled at the alpha menacingly until he had backed off.

Choosing to leave the female to her task, he left the shelter of the den and scented the air, his breaths sending out cotton clouds of fog that dissipated quickly in the chilling breeze. He took a moment to stretch his big body its full length and flexing his tightened muscles to their limits. Then he shook himself beginning with his massive head and ending at his rump. Sensing that his mate didn't want him around, he began moving swiftly away from the den and through the forest until he once again came within sight of the cabin. Concealed in the gloom of the forest, he lay down, his cold, blue eyes never leaving the porch. He paused, his body tense and alert. He didn't know what he was waiting for, but his body trembled with excitement. For now, he was content to wait. Resting his big head on his front paws, he began his vigil again.

Chapter Twenty-One

An hour after the alpha male had left the den, the she-wolf began having severe abdominal contractions. As before, she lay still, her breathing short and coming in gasps. When the urge hit her, she would instinctively push hard, but this time she could sense that there something was wrong. The progress of this pup's birth was infinitely different than the other three had been. The pain was much worse and the pup wasn't moving as easily through the birth canal. In fact, it wasn't moving at all. With each new contraction, the dam whimpered against the increasing pain in frustration, but her natural birth instinct made her continue to push harder to force the whelp out as quickly as possible. Before long a greenish black, foul-smelling discharge began to leak from the dam's vagina indicating that the baby wasn't viable. Her body was trying to expel the dead puppy, but she no longer had the strength to push. Unable to force the fetus to move any further along the canal, the mother began to tremble and convulse. Spittle ran out her mouth and her eyes rolled back into their sockets. Her weakened efforts to express the corpse from her womb left her physically exhausted. Laying down her head, she closed her eyes and succumbed to the inevitable. Within minutes she is dead, the unborn fetus having never arrived. The dam's body cooled rapidly in the bitter cold, and without their mother's body heat to keep them toasty warm, the three newborn pups began to whine and frantically work to huddle closer together in a desperate attempt to find warmth. Unfortunately, without their mother to protect them, it isn't long before they also perished in the freezing temperatures.

Over a mile away, the alpha male sat up. There had been no activity around the structure and his need to feed filled his being. He knew that he needed to find food soon. Not just for himself, but also for his mate who would need food after giving birth to the litter. He walked deeper into the aspen growth letting his strong sense of smell lead the way. The bitterly cold weather had forced all potential prey to remain hidden safely in their homes, and the hungry wolf eventually had no option, but to once again return to the den empty-handed. However, as he comes within sight of the lair, he sensed something was off and paused to survey the surroundings. Seeing nothing to account for his uneasiness, he moves forward cautiously to the cave entrance. Once there, he was hit with a noxious odor and he guardedly drew nearer to his mate and new family.

Sniffing at the dead female, he tried to get a reaction from her by licking her face roughly with his tongue. When this produced no results, he used his head to butt against her body, but again, she didn't move or make a sound. Using one of his massive paws, he tried to illicit a response, but his actions only cause one of the frozen puppies to roll away from the mother. The big grey finally accepted the fact that his mate and all of his offspring are gone. Backing out of the den, he sat back on his haunches and released a long, deep, mournful howl that carried far through the clear, crisp morning air calling the rest of the pack back to the lair.

Chapter Twenty-Two

Dressed again in his winter gear, Ben kicked a path back through the deep snow until he reached the equipment shed. After several minutes of clearing enough snow from in front of the big doors, he finally managed to slide them open wide. He went in and pulled off the canvas tarp covering the snow cat. Taking the rifle from his shoulder, he slid it into the scabbard he had attached to the machine the previous night. After doing a quick check to make sure that his pistol was fully loaded and he had everything he thought he would need, he climbed aboard and started the engine. It instantly came to life with a steady powerful thrum that broke the pristine silence of the morning and sent a flock of white-winged crossbills soaring high into the grey sky. Checking one last time that his pistol was fully loaded, he turned the purring beast through the doors and out into the snow. Ben liked the feel of the powerful engine as he straddled the leather seat. Throttling back on the RPMs, the man eased the snowmobile further onto the snow pack. Pointing the large metal beast toward the southeast, man and machine began moving easily over the deep snow. Maneuvering the snow cat through the dense forest was slow going because of brush and boulders that were hidden by the snowfall, but he kept going. He knew that he needed to get to Becca as soon as he could, but that wasn't going to happen if he damaged their only means of escape by running into a tree or breaking a ski on some half-buried rock. So, he continued to move forward with caution. He could feel his muscles tighten up with tension over the painfully slow pace he was moving, but it couldn't be helped. Sometime later the quiet of the woodland was once again shattered, but this time by a lonesome howl that chilled Ben to his very bones. He paused the snow cat only a minute before pushing on. It had almost sounded like a wounded animal, and ordinarily, he would have gone to investigate, but it seemed more like an omen of things to come. Besides, today his primary attention was reaching Becca.

Although it was no longer snowing, the frigid temperature and the snow being kicked up by the machine quickly caused ice crystals to form on Ben's snow goggles and in his beard. From time to time, he found it necessary to stop and wipe the glaze off the glasses so he could see more clearly. Still, he remained focused on his destination and after almost two hours of traveling, he finally broke free of the forest and into the open meadow. He could just make out the small cabin at the far end of the lea with gray smoke escaping up the chimney and coloring the clear sky like a smudged fingerprint on a windowpane. He let the big machine idle while he paused just long enough to clean off his goggles once again before moving forward again. He wanted to make sure that his vision wasn't impaired in any way that might hinder him from seeing the wolves approaching.

From inside the log cabin, Becca heard the faint sounds of an engine. It was obviously still far away, but her heart swelled with excitement realizing that it had to be Ben coming to their rescue and they would finally be able to leave this place of nightmares. Not wanting to venture outside the protection of the cabin until absolutely necessary, she nonetheless moved to the front window to try and determine exactly where the sound was coming for. Unfortunately, the window didn't provide her with a large enough view of the area. Disappointed, she realized she would just have to be patient with the knowledge that help was clearly on its way.

Ben was very pleased that the first part of his journey was nearly over and shortly he would be meeting Becca in person. He could do with a steaming cup of joe and a chance to rest after the bone-jarring trip. In his mind's eye, he tried to envision what he thought Becca might look like and allowed himself to fantasize their first meeting. He'd thought about her a lot over the past several days. Smiling, he pictured her throwing herself into his arms and showering him with grateful kisses while Sadie jumped around them barking happily. Okay, he knew this wasn't likely going to happen, but hey, it was *his* dream after all, wasn't it? At the very least, maybe she'd have that hot cup of strong coffee he was dying for waiting for him.

Temporarily lost in his woolgathering, he failed to see the flash of grey and white fur until it was already upon him. With a growl and teeth bared, the massive wolf slammed into his side, knocking him completely off the snowmobile and land face down in the snow. The big gray's momentum had carried it further past the prone body of the ranger, but it immediately got to its feet, turned back and bit onto his right arm. The thickness of his insulated jacket prevented the viciously curved canines to go deep enough to do more than scratch his flesh, but the pressure from the powerful jaws felt as if his arm was caught in a vice. As good as it was, Ben knew that he wouldn't be able to count on the protection of his jacket for long. In the meantime, his heart skipped as he looked up and saw two smaller wolves charging at him from the shadow of the woods. Upon reaching Ben, the new pair began ferociously attacking him, as well. Their jaws snapped and slaver was sent flying as the helpless young man desperately tried to fend off all three wolves with only his hands. The sheer brutal strength of the alpha allowed him to drag the 270 pound man several feet from the sled as it continued to rip and tear through the heavy material of Ben's coat. In seconds, the wolf had reached his now exposed arm. Ben screamed in agony as blood ran out of the newly opened wound and the large crimson drops fell from the ranger's arm and colored the snowy ground around him. At that moment, Notch-Ear latched onto Ben's shoulder, barely missing his neck, but managing to seize the fabric ripping a large piece of the collar completely off.

Ben's hood had fallen back during the struggle, and Notch-Ear took immediate advantage by changing direction and lunging straight at the ranger's face. Ben saw the attack coming, and at the last second raised his left arm up to protect his exposed skin. Unfortunately, the action wasn't fast enough. Snapping and snarling, the wolf's fangs carved a four inch slice along his cheek before Ben managed to avert his face from more damage. Not to be put off, Notch-Ear turned back and sank his teeth deeply into the ranger's gloved hand. The fangs easily sliced through the fabric and blood now flowed freely from both his hand and the gaping gash on his face.

"Argh," Ben cried out as he struggled against the violent onslaught. His body was screaming in pain and still he was unable to break free. He understood that unless he was able to get loose, he would very likely wind up like his friend, Sammy Dix.

The smaller and lighter female wolf chose to avoid Ben's flailing arms and instead, viciously assaulted Ben's left thigh. This particular area had only the slight protection of his snowsuit, and so was easier for her to attack. Her sharp teeth tore through the insulated material and sunk deeply into the vulnerable soft flesh of his upper thigh. Ben screamed out loud from this new torture as she shook her head back and forth violently until she finally was able to tear off a two-inch chunk of meat.

Covered in blood from all of his wounds, Ben let out a loud "Oof" as a heavy weight landed squarely on top of his back forcing all of the wind out of his lungs with a whoosh. Ben knew it was the alpha male again and also understood that if the beast managed to get hold of his neck, he would be dead within seconds. He had to get loose! He had to find a weapon! Using all the strength he could muster, he ripped his hand free from the mouth of Notch-Ear leaving the bloody glove caught in the teeth. Then using the injured hand, he pushed himself up and rolled over. The sudden and unexpected movement caught the bigger wolf unprepared, and he rolled along with the ranger, falling to the side. Using this momentary advantage, Ben began to drag himself back towards the snow cat being careful not to make any sudden moves that might set the alpha off again.

The two smaller wolves had released their holds on the man as well, and now ran around him in a frenetic attack, barking and taking quick painful nips at any exposed areas they could see. When he finally made it to the machine, Ben reached up into the open compartment and withdrew one of the emergency flares he had put there earlier.

Striking it alight, he used the flare to ward off the wolves' attacks as he inched even closer to the rifle. The smaller wolves backed off being careful to stay out of range of the flame while still aggressively snarling and charging at him. At one point, sparks from the flare touched the female's nose causing her to yelp in pain. The alpha male stood a few feet away breathing heavily and watched as the wounded man edged even nearer to the leather scabbard. His stone cold eyes never left the man and he gnashed his teeth together. Just as Ben was reaching up to unstrap the rifle from the scabbard, the flare he had been holding sputtered out and the alpha sprang forward. He bit down hard on Ben's left shoulder near the spot Notch-Ear had mangled earlier. When Ben turned his head to see what had happened, he was shocked to find himself staring directly into the face of a monster. Its ice blue eyes stared back and held nothing, but savage malevolence directed at the ranger. Black lips were drawn back allowing Ben to see just how large and deadly those teeth were. Blood coated its snout and saliva ran from the ranger's shoulder down his arm, and still the wolf hung on tenaciously. The ranger's heart was filled with fear, because he was beginning to understand that his chance of surviving this battle of wills was not looking good.

He could already feel his body weakening due to the loss of blood, and using what little strength he had left he managed to reach under his anorak and take hold of his Buck knife. As he brought it out, the younger male resumed his attack and leapt at the ranger. The sunlight reflected off the blade like a laser beam as Ben swung widely. He managed to catch the bigger male with an eight inch long, deep slice that ran along his side instantly drawing blood that stained his beautiful silver gray fur the color of rust. The alpha howled in pain and temporarily released his hold on the man. Bringing the knife back again, he sank it deeply into the throat of Notch-Ear just as the young male was about to attack him again. Thick, hot blood showered Ben's face and shoulder as the artery continued to pump out the wolf's lifeblood. The beta threw back its head and gave a short wail before falling off to the side. Ben's strength was ebbing fast. He couldn't hold onto the knife and the critically injured wolf carried it with him leaving Ben without a weapon. Its legs of the beta male continued to kick uselessly for several seconds before death finally took him.

The alpha male had also been severely injured, but its intense hatred of the man pushed him onward and it managed to fall back upon Ben, thrusting its enormous head towards the ranger's face. The man gasped as he watched the wolf's bloodied muzzle coming at him, its mouth drawn back in a gory grimace. Out of sheer desperation, Ben reached up and grabbed the fur on either side of the wide open maw to try and hold the canine off him, but his strength was fading steadily and by this time, the fingers of his injured hand had very little feeling left in them at all. The wolf, sensing his victim's strength diminishing, lunged once more for the man's neck. At the last moment, however, Ben turned his head and the wolf's teeth scraped along the soft flesh. While this maneuver resulted in opening fresh superficial wounds along the man's chin and neck, the big wolf was only able to bite down onto the neck of the coat rather than the man's vulnerable throat.

Frustrated, the alpha threw back his head and let loose with a primal roar of rage. Then it returned to savagely attacking the heavy material that was blocking it from reaching the tender flesh underneath. Shaking his massive head back and forth like a dog with a bone, insulation and fabric flew in every direction. In his weakened state, Ben was viciously jerked back and forth like a rag doll. He was pushing as hard as he could on the big wolf with his right hand, when he became aware that the female wolf had managed to tear off his boot and was now brutally attacking his foot. Blood and gore immediately soaked his sock. Ben didn't know how much longer he would be able to stand the pain his body was experiencing, so with the last of his strength he reached down and grabbed the loose skin on the neck of the female. With a herculean effort, he wrenched the bitch away and roughly threw the smaller wolf to the side where she hit the side of the sled hard. He could see she was still breathing, but she was bleeding from a wound on her head and she didn't get up again.

Temporarily distracted, Ben gasped when he felt teeth tear off his earlobe as the alpha tried again to reach the vulnerable flesh at his throat. He jerked his head back, causing blood to fly across his face in the process. His strength was all but gone, and he knew he wouldn't be able to fight off the big wolf for very much longer. He was so tired. He would die without ever having been able to meet Becca. Tears began to fall as the wolf continued to assault him.

He needn't have worried, though. Wondering why she was no longer able to hear the sound of the snow cat's engine, Becca had ventured out onto the porch while the attack by the pack was in its full fury. The brutality of the scene was horrifying, and she had frozen in fear as the wolves continued their attack on the man. Ben saw the stunned woman and knew she would be no match for the wolf once he took notice of her. He had to do something and it had to be now before it was too late.

"Becca!" Ben screamed with all of the volume his voice could manage. "Becca, please. You need to get back inside! Do it now! Please, Becca! Go!"

The pain and panic that Becca heard in his voice shocked her back into the moment, and she screamed at the giant wolf with all of her might, "STOP IT! Get away from him!" Not realizing what she was doing, she started running in the direction of the carnage and the abhorrent beast, her falling tears freezing on her cheeks.

At the sound of her voice, the big wolf released his grip on the man and turned toward the sound of her voice. Its cold blue eyes immediately locked on her teary green ones. He knew he was looking at his true enemy. This human was the one who had hurt him with the iron stick. This human had been responsible for blinding his mate, and it had been this human who had prevented him from reaching the bitch in heat. His rage boiled with renewed ferocity. In his weakened state, Ben was hardly able to do more than try and grab uselessly at the creature's wet fur to try and prevent it from moving in Becca's direction. The alpha, however, was having none of it. Leaving the ravaged ranger covered in blood where he lay, the massive wolf turned toward the woman. The massive wound on its side still leaked, and its muzzle and coat were drenched in blood from both the ranger's injuries and his own, but it lowered its head keeping its eyes on its quarry and began to walk slowly, but deliberately in the direction of Becca. It was in no real hurry. It understood that even injured, he was still more powerful that this particular human.

Ben continued to whisper Becca's name like a prayer. "Please, God. Please protect her."

Becca felt a moment of relief when she saw the massive wolf release the ranger from its grip, until she realized that he was now coming towards her! The wolf was covered in blood and strings of bloody slobber dripped from his mouth. Whether the blood was his or Ben's she couldn't tell, and at the moment, she didn't care. The hostility coming off the alpha was a near physical thing, and realizing she had no weapon to protect herself with, she began to back away. When Becca reached the cabin steps, she turned to go inside, but when she opened the door, she was unexpectedly knocked off balance by a sudden streak of black fur. With a snarl on her face and barking loudly, Sadie charged past her startled mistress and bolted directly towards the much larger male wolf. Becca stared in horror as the wolf immediately began to run towards the smaller canine with its teeth bared. Like two bighorn sheep vying for dominance, the pair smashed into each other in a head-on frenzy of teeth, fur and blood.

"Oh, my god," Becca mourned aloud. She knew that her loving canine companion was absolutely no match for the huge silver beast and her heart broke. She had to find a way to fight back; to save Sadie and hopefully, Ben as well. Hiding in the cabin would only delay the inevitable and Ben would likely die, too, if he wasn't dead already. She could hear the painful yelps coming from Sadie as she tried to maintain the fight with a beast twice her size, but Becca knew it was only a matter of time. Looking around her, her eyes fell on the abandoned patrol car sitting in the yard. A desperate hope began to grow inside her as she prayed that she might be able to find a weapon of some sort inside the car. As the vicious battle between dog and wolf continued, Becca opened the passenger door and threw herself into the car. The dead trooper's blood had frozen and it crackled under the woman's weight as she climbed in. Becca began searching for something – anything! - that she could use to defend herself. Frantically searching through the glove compartment and under the seats, she was unable to find anything useful. A sudden sharp yelp of pain from the direction of the dog fight caused her to look up through the safety glass. The alpha male was standing with its feet apart holding Sadie's broken neck in its mouth, but he was looking directly at Becca. Clouds of vapor billowed out of the wolf with each breath it took. Dropping the body of her beloved pet, the wolf shook its head as if dismissing the whole incident the way he would a bothersome fly and began to once more move in her direction. Its silver-gray fur was nearly completely hidden beneath a layer of blood. Some of it his, some of it Sadie's, and undoubtedly, some of it was Ben's. Sadie's brutalized body now lay motionless in the blood-soaked snow. Tears coursed freely down her cheeks even as anger filled Becca at the loss of her pet. Sadie had given her life to protect Becca and she made a silent promise to Sadie that it wouldn't be a waste. She was not going to give up! No one else was going to die because of this monster! More determined than ever to kill the beast, or die trying, Becca searched under the seats in vain for anything she could use to fend off the relentless attacker.

Almost ready to resign herself to a terrifying fate, she happen to glance out the open driver's door and saw something black and metallic barely sticking upright in the snow just outside the door. Recognizing it for what it was, she quickly crawled to the door and reached down to retrieve Trooper Dix's service weapon. With renewed fortitude, Becca sat up and swung her legs out of the auto. Standing behind the open driver's side door in a foot of cold, wet snow, Becca shivered. She had not bothered to put on her coat when she had left the cabin, but now the cold was secondary. She was simply too full of hate and vengeance to allow it into her thoughts. Still moving slowly, but deliberately, the wolf had moved to within a hundred feet of the car when it suddenly broke into a run. Its lips were drawn back revealing the sharp white teeth set in black gums as it quickly closed the distance between them. Its gaze never left Becca's until she raised the pistol. Something in the wolf's memory recognized the power of the weapon and he stopped advancing, but he was too filled with blood lust to hesitate for very long.

Becca felt a sudden calmness wash over her as she stepped around the car door and aimed the pistol at the oncoming beast. She had not held a gun since she had last been hunting with her dad years before, and then it had been a rifle. She could almost hear his deep voice giving instructions to her as she corrected her stance, took careful aim, drew in a big breath and fired the pistol several times. The first two bullets missed their target cleanly, kicking up snow near the charging wolf. The third one grazed the wolf's shoulder, causing him to jump like he had just been stung by a wasp. Bewildered by what had just happened, the alpha stopped in his tracks to lick the wound briefly. Still determined to reach the woman who had already been the cause of so much pain, he began moving forward again, but this time much more cautiously. Blood ran freely from the wound on his side from Ben's knife and from where the bullet had hit him. No less focused on Becca, the big male had moved to within fifty feet before the woman fired again. This bullet hit the wolf directly in the center of its chest and the beast collapsed in the snow. The creature didn't attempt to rise, but Becca could still see its clouds of fog as his broad chest continued rising and falling with each breath.

The woman approached the big wolf warily. She knew that an injured animal could be even more deadly and she honestly didn't know how badly hurt it was. When she was still a couple of feet from it, the huge wolf turned his immense head to look back at her. Eyes the color of the summer sky stared at her, only now she could see that they were filled with pain, not hostility. Even through his agony, he was still defiant, and drew back his lips to snarl threateningly at the woman. Unwavering, Becca raised the pistol and took careful aim. "This one's for Sadie, you bastard," she whispered as she pulled the trigger. The sound of that final gunshot echoed through the little valley as the bullet entered the wolf's head. The beast was finally dead.

Chapter Twenty-Three

As the warm blood began to spread around the body, it melted the snow turning it from white to pink. Becca was amazed by just how large the animal actually was. Even she had to admit that it was an impressive and beautiful beast, but it <u>had</u> been a beast and it had been deadly. Letting the pistol fall beside the inert body, Becca ran over the fallen ranger. He was covered in blood and wasn't moving at all.

Dropping to her knees, her heart rose into her throat. "He's so still," she thought. "Oh, God, please let him still be alive."

Seeing his blue lips moving silently, she fell to her knees next to the injured man. Leaning in closely, she could just make out a whispered, "Becca". Her heart leapt with joy and she gently brushed a bloody lock of sandy hair off his forehead. Her joy only grew when she saw him open his beautiful blue eyes and look up at her. A relieved smile spreading across her tear-stained face, she said, "Hi, Ben. I'm Becca."

Ben gave her a lopsided grin, grimaced from the pain that small movement caused, and came back with, "Sorry I can't get up, but it's nice to finally meet you."

Becca took his hand in both of hers and seriously asked, "Tell me what I need to do for you?"

Swallowing hard, Ben told her to use the radio in the patrol car to contact the authorities. Before doing what he had said, Becca took two of the blankets off the sled and covered the ranger to keep him from going into shock. Then she ran as fast as she could back to the SUV. Picking up the radio mike, she began frantically trying to reach someone at the other end. It took several seconds for her to understand she had to press the button on the mike in order to broadcast and release it to listen.

"Help! Hello? Is anyone listening? Please, someone, please answer me! We've been attacked by wolves and there is a ranger who is very badly hurt. " Desperation and panic caused her voice to rise in pitch and volume as if by talking louder she could make someone hear her without the radio. She knew that if Ben didn't get medical help soon, he could still die from the loss of blood and exposure. She clicked the mike several times and tried again. This time she was rewarded by a response.

"Hello, this is the dispatcher," the calm voice came over the speaker said. "You are not authorized to be on this frequency. Who is this?"

"Thank God," Becca thought, but she said "My name is Rebecca Thornton. We've been attacked by wolves. A highway patrolman is dead and the forest ranger that came to help has been mauled badly and lost a lot of blood. He needs medical attention as soon as possible."

Becca went on to give the dispatcher details on where they were located and explained how she happened to be speaking on the patrol car's radio. The dispatcher confirmed that due to the highway closures, a normal ambulance would be unable to reach them. He had, however, already requested an emergency medical helicopter be dispatched and it should be arriving within minutes. Before signing off, he suggested that Becca return to the injured man and try to keep him conscious and as comfortable as she could until the medical team arrived. Dropping the now useless microphone, Becca raced into the cabin, grabbed her coat and another blanket from the bunk room before running back to Ben. As she returned, she passed the broken body of Sadie. Her eyes grew wet, but she knew there was nothing she could do for her friend. Right now Ben needed her full attention. She only hoped that Sadie would understand.

When she reached him again, she was shocked to see how much paler he seemed. Taking care to not move him too quickly, she raised his head and placed the folded blanket under his head. Ben moaned, but didn't cry out. He was breathing shallowly now. A loose flap of skin hung from his face where the wolf had clawed him, but it appeared that the bleeding had slowed. That was something, at least.

Stroking his hair, she said, "They're coming, Ben. They'll be here soon." Fresh tears were falling as she said, "Just keep holding on and don't go to sleep."

"So tired. So cold," was his reply.

"I know you are, but I need to stay with me. Hold onto my hand. I won't let you go."

Ben looked into her incredible green eyes and nodded weakly.

The sound of a helicopter approaching reached Becca and she covered Ben's face with her hand to protect it from the flying snow and debris as the copter landed nearby. Two men jumped out of the side door before it had even landed and were running towards them as the rotors slowed.

"Ben, the helicopter's here. You're going to be fine." She prayed that she was telling him the truth.

"You'll have to move back, ma'am," the young medic said as he opened his case and removed a blood pressure cuff, which he quickly placed around Ben's arm. As it electronically took a reading, the medic went about checking the extent of his wounds efficiently and quickly.

"No, I've got to stay." Becca cried. "I promised him I wouldn't let go of his hand."

A strong hand touched her shoulder from behind her and a gruff, but gentle voice said, "It's going to be okay, miss. You've done a great job for Ben so far, but now you have to let the doctor do his."

Becca turned and looked up at the man. He looked to be in his early 60's with thick salt and pepper hair blowing wildly around his face. His tanned and weathered skin had obviously seen many years of being in out the elements, but his blue eyes were kind and bright with intelligence. The brown uniform he wore indicated to Becca that he, too, worked for the Forestry Service. His name tag read "Hank". Reaching down, he placed a large, rough hand beneath her elbow and helped her to rise. Pulling Becca with him, the ranger stepped back to allow a second medic carrying a stretcher move in closer to Ben's side. She watched as the pair attached an IV to Ben's arm and injected something into the line. Then they carefully lifted him onto the canvas. Ben moaned loudly.

"BP is 87 over 56. We've gotta move fast," the first medic said and the pair raced to the waiting chopper carrying Ben between them. Becca started to move after them, but the older ranger held her back.

Becca looked into his kind face as he told her, "There isn't enough room for us in the chopper and we'd only be in their way. I know you want to go with him, and if that were an option, I would tell you to go for it. But, right now he's exactly where he needs to be with the people who can best take care of him. Besides, we need to take the sled back to headquarters and then I promise I'll take you straight to the hospital from there."

She looked at the man and nodded mutely. In her heart, she understood that whether or not Ben survived the attack, there was nothing more that she could do for him. She turned to watch as the rotors began to turn and the sleds left the ground. She could see the two doctors working quickly, covering Ben's face with an oxygen mask and giving him another injection. One of the medics looked up at her as he reached over and slammed the door hard. The copter took off in a whirlwind of ice crystals, brushing the tops of the pines as it passed overhead. When it was no longer in sight, the ranger left her and began readying the snow cat for the trip back to the ranger station. Becca stood silently by and watched him tip the machine back on its skis. When he picked up the wolf with the piece of its ear missing and threw the body unceremoniously into the cargo sled, she felt nothing. Then she turned and walked briskly back to the cabin, returning with Sadie's blanket. Carrying the well-worn piece of fabric, she went directly over to her dead pet and knelt down beside her. Stroking the soft black fur, her tears began to fall in earnest, but she briskly wiped them away with the sleeve of her coat. Taking the faded blanket in her hands, she wrapped it around the body and standing, she reached down to lift the dog. Sadie's body had stiffened slightly from the freezing cold and she was much heavier than Becca realized.

"Let me," came the soft, caring voice of the older ranger as he bent down. The girl looked into his kind eyes and stepped back. Hank easily lifted Sadie into his arms like she was a child and started back the way he had just come.

With Becca leading the way, the pair reached the snow cat and Becca climbed on board. She chose to sit on the bench. Without being told to do so, the ranger laid the body of Sadie next to her so that her smooth black head was cradled in Becca's lap. Folding back the corner of the blanket, Becca lovingly stroked the soft head of her faithful protector. Her chocolate eyes were now closed as if she was sleeping and Becca allowed her fresh tears to fall unchecked. With one last look back at his passenger, the ranger started up the machine and moved forward toward the big alpha male.

He brought the powerful machine alongside the beast. Leaving the motor idling, he struggled to heft the massive animal onto the cargo sled beside its smaller companion. Then he climbed back on board and began to maneuver the snow cat back the way Ben had brought it in. It would be easy to follow the obvious tracks left in the snow all the way to the ranger headquarters.

"There was a third one," came the quiet voice from behind him.

The ranger stopped the snow cat and turned to look at the young woman. "I'm sorry, miss. Did you say something?"

Becca brought her glittering green eyes up to look directly into his and spoke again, but louder. "Three wolves attacked Ben. I saw them. What happened to the third one?"

The ranger put the cat in park and climbed off. He spent the next several minutes scanning the whole open area, but there were so many tracks and so much blood that he was unable to determine where the missing wolf had gone. Mounting the snow machine, he faced the young woman and replied, "Likely was just injured and dragged itself back into the woods to die. No need to worry about it now. I need to get you back to the outpost where you can warm up."

Big wet flakes were once again beginning to fall as the old ranger began to move the big snow machine back toward the forest. The grey sky threatened and Becca's mood was no better.

Chapter Twenty-Four
April 5th
Silver Dollar Ranch

Becca lazily swept off the dirt and leaves that had collected on the wide veranda of guest cabin #3 as she hummed a random tune. Two new families were expected to arrive later today and she had to make sure that everything was ready for their arrival. The working ranch was spread out over 175 acres of virgin forest and pasture land. The Silver Dollar Lodge and guest cabins were perfectly situated within a small mountain valley so that they overlooked a swift-moving tributary of the Colorado River that emptied into a good sized lake located on the property. Sunlight danced across its tranquil surface as the images of white clouds moved silently overhead. Stocked regularly with trout, the fish broke the water periodically in their effort to catch the sparkling sunbeams reflected there. The clear blue-green water offered residents at the ranch another activity option during their time stay.

Dressed in her favorite outfit of straight-legged jeans, a well-worn flannel shirt over a black tee, and a pair of dust covered cowboy boots, Becca paused in her work to remove the baseball cap she had on and shake out her thick auburn hair. There was still an early morning chill in the air, but it would warm up quickly throughout the day. The smell of new grass and the blooming wildflowers offered a heady bouquet. Becca closed her eyes to savor the way the gentle breeze caressed her skin and lifted random tendrils of her hair to brush across her face. Resting the broom against the porch railing, she threw a hip onto the porch railing and sat to look out over the sprawling ranch. <u>Her</u> ranch now. She was never disappointed by the stunning beauty of the Rocky Mountains. Even though snow was still possible at this time of year and drifts could still be found in the shadowy areas and on top of Old Baldy. An explosion of Larkspur, Columbine, Buttercups and a myriad of other wildflowers painted the landscape like they were done with an artist's hand. Day before yesterday, she had been delighted to watch a family of deer coming out from the forest to drink from the creek that ran through her valley.

    Shading her eyes with her hand, she could just make out her foreman, Floyd, and some of his crew rounding up the horses that had wandered to the far end of the canyon. The newest guests would no doubt want to go for a trail ride later in the day – they always did – and so the hands needed to bring up several of the more gentle ponies and put them in the corral. The smell of fresh baked bread wafted in the air and Becca took a deep breath. Frieda was obviously busy in the kitchen baking pies and working on pulling tonight's meal together. Nothing gourmet, but she was gifted at making the kind of delicious comfort food that really stuck to your ribs. Homemade Lasagna, broth rich Chicken and Dumplings, and brook trout fresh from the river and then stuffed with a Cajun cornbread dressing were staples on the menu with an occasional venison roast thrown in. The couple had been a true Godsend for Becca since her arrival, and she was the first to admit that she would never have been able to manage things without their expansive knowledge and experience. Slightly overwhelmed at first, under their combined (and patient) guidance, Becca had quickly learned the ins and outs of running a working guest ranch.

Now that spring in the mountains had officially returned and Mother Nature was working her magic to painting everything a rich, vibrant green and the breeze was full of floral perfume, Becca was surprised and delighted to see how quickly the reservations were starting to come in. According to the office calendar, they were already completely booked through July and the first part of August. This was no small feat in and of itself as the ranch offered twenty individual cabins of various sizes that could house anywhere from four to 10 comfortably. Each unit had a fully functional and well-supplied kitchen, bath, and wood-burning fireplace. The nights on the Divide could be cold even during the summer and snow could still fall all the way into late July, so those simple conveniences were welcomed by the visitors who came to stay for a while. Each cabin was decorated in warm colors and soft linens. Becca had made it her personal responsibility to make sure that every unit offered their guests a cozy, welcoming place to put their feet up after a long day of fishing or trekking the mountains.

The main floor of the lodge was made up of the kitchen, the dining hall – which was an option open to all guests of the ranch – and a recreation hall that was large enough to hold a regulation-sized pool table, a ping pong table, two game tables where guests were able to play anything from solitaire to a raucous game of penny-ante poker, two pinball machines, and a comfortable lounge area where guests could simply sit back and relax in front of the huge fieldstone fireplace. A 72 inch television screen was hung above the mantle and every Saturday night the ranch featured a classic movie for the enjoyment of their guests, complete with popcorn and candy. As the nearest movie theater was clear down in South Fork, many guests from other nearby ranches often joined in the fun on Saturday nights. This week's cinematic treat was going to be *The Alamo* with John Wayne, a personal favorite of Becca's father. Truth be told, the classic movie was one of her favorites, too.

One of the first additions that Becca made upon her arrival was to add a small convenience store off to the left of the main lobby. This twenty foot by twenty-five foot space was able to provide those items visitors and guest might have forgotten to bring along. Snacks of all kinds - bread, lunch meat, milk, sodas, ice cream, personal toiletries, candy bars and a variety of other items and souvenirs were for sale, including natural honey harvested directly from the hives located on the ranch itself. With no other grocery options available for miles on either side of the Divide, this had actually become quite popular with anyone staying at the ranch, as well as passing fishermen, campers, and sightseers visiting the general area.

The second floor of the lodge held eight additional guest suites. These were typically taken by travelers who only needed a place to stay for one or two nights, but it wasn't unheard of for those transient guests who had planned to only stay overnight wound up staying for week. Breakfast and dinner were included in the price of each suite, leaving the middle of the day open for exploring the mountains and visiting local sites of interest. Picnic lunches could be purchased for those guests who wanted to bask in the natural beauty of the mountains and hike their hidden glens.

The entire third floor of the lodge belonged solely to Becca and was off limits to all guests. Her parents had created it to be their own private retreat where they could retire after a long day on the ranch and virtually leave the world outside their closed door. The space included its own gourmet kitchen, a large open living area with a huge fireplace made from river rocks, an office, two guest bedrooms with full baths, a master suite with its own fireplace, and a private balcony that overlooked the valley. This was Becca's favorite spot on the whole ranch and she spent as much time as she possibly could sitting in one of the comfortable Adirondack chairs sipping wine or hot chocolate – depending on the weather - as she watched the glorious morning sunrises and spectacular star-studded evenings. It was also at these quiet times that Becca could almost feel her parents standing on either side of her and she was completely at peace.

Since escaping the horrifying experience with the wolves, everything in her life had been going so smoothly. Her mother had finally been laid to rest the week after she and Ben had been rescued. She now lay next to Becca's father in the family plot situated in a secluded tree-shaded glade on the ranch itself overlooking the valley. The area was filled with the fragrance of lavender and wild birdsong. Hidden within the protective copse of her great grandfather's beloved quaking silver aspen, Becca made it a point to take time out every week to spend time there.

Since her arrival at the ranch, she amazed herself by how little she actually missed the big city. There was no doubt that the responsibilities of the ranch kept her jumping, but she truly felt like she had come home. Her biweekly forays into Creede or Lake City for supplies were like mini adventures. She always enjoyed never knowing what she might see around the next bend in the road, whether that be catching the flight of an eagle as it glided on the thermals or watching the rain as it moved down through the valley. Brown bears and big horn sheep could be seen wandering above the tree line and formations of Canadian geese often dotted the sky.

Noticing a cloud of dust moving up the drive, Becca replaced her cap and squinted in the bright midday sun. Could one of the expected guests have arrived earlier that they had planned? Check-in was officially three P.M., but she would never refuse a guest who arrived sooner than expected. Didn't really matter, anyway, because she knew everything was ready for their arrival. Leaning the broom back against the wall of the huge log cabin, Becca brushed the dust from her hands and stepped down off the porch. Now that the car was closer, she could tell that it was a dark green Chevy Trailblazer and her face immediately broke into a huge smile. After the nightmare situation that had taken place in January, she and ranger Ben had become close friends. In fact, it was safe to say that they were much closer than just friends now. Her heart began to beat faster just thinking about him.

The injuries he had suffered at the hands (or paws) of the wild wolf pack had been substantial and he had to be hospitalized for several weeks while he healed. He had needed over fifty stitches for the various wounds on his face and hands, but surgery and several skin grafts were called for to repair the extensive damage done to his leg. In spite of some intense physical therapy, he still only had limited mobility, and he had to depend on a cane to get around. It was this that had forced him to leave the forestry service. While he was recuperating in the hospital, Becca had visited her hero every day, and once in a while she would see Hank there, too. There had never been any shyness between Ben and Becca, even when they had first met face to face on that frozen January day. It had always been so natural between them, relaxed and comfortable. So much had happened to them that there had been no awkwardness to deal with. Once the doctors released him to go home, Becca had picked him up from the hospital and Ben had immediately asked her to go dinner with him at Antlers Riverside Restaurant as he had promised her. She had accepted without hesitation, and the pair had been together ever since. They happily discovered that they both like classic westerns, collecting Indian arrowheads, professional football – although they routed for different teams – and thick lemon custard.

The SUV came to a sliding stop on the loose gravel in front of the lodge and Ben climbed out. His leg had apparently stiffened some during the drive, because he moved slowly and with difficulty. The doctors assured him that it was only temporary as his muscles mended, and it wouldn't be long before he was as mobile as ever. Becca didn't wait for him to come to her, but ran up and threw her arms around his neck instead.

Holding her in his arms, he said with a slightly cockeyed boyish grin as he tipped his head to the right, "Careful. Your guests might be watching."

Shaking her head emphatically, she responded, "No chance. They haven't arrived yet and even if they were, I'm not ashamed. They would just have to deal with it."

With a grin, Ben lowered his head as Becca stood on the toes of his Doc Martins and kissed him long and hard. When they broke apart, she took his face in her hands and looked directly into his chocolate brown eyes. Momentarily struck by the similarity of his and Sadie's beautiful brown eyes, she whispered, "I've missed you so much," her voice husky with passion.

"We just saw each other yesterday!" Ben laughed.

"I know, but I've gotten used to having you nearby and besides, it gets a really lonely around here at night," she said smiling up at him coyly.

Standing to his full height, he grinned broadly and said, "Well, I have something that just might fix that problem! Stay here for just a minute. I'll be right back with a surprise, so close your eyes!" Halfway to the car, he turned back yelling, "And no peeking!"

Becca closed her eyes and laughed as Ben walked to the back of his car. She heard him opening the rear hatch, and begin to mess around with something there. Then he slammed the door shut and came around the side of the car. Walking beside him was a young yellow lab with a huge red bow tied around its neck. In the way all pups have, his eyes were bright with excitement taking in everything around him at once and his pink tongue hung out of the side of his mouth dripping saliva into the dirt. Its tail was wagging so fiercely that it whipped against Ben's trouser leg. Still a few feet from Becca, Ben stopped suddenly. He pulled back slightly on the leash and the dog immediately sat down in the dirt.

"You can open your eyes now, Becca."

Becca blinked in the bright sun as her eyes focused on the sight in front of her. She was stunned and stared open-mouthed at the dog for a few seconds before running forward to greet the excited pup. Falling to her knees in front of him, she squealed with delight. "Oh, Ben! He's beautiful! Thank you so much."

"I know that he could never replace Sadie, but I figured that you needed a big brave man around the place to protect you from any menacing field mice and those always hostile chipmunks."

Smiling up at Ben while the pup happily licked her face, Becca said, "Well, we'll definitely have to work on that, won't we?"

Enduring a seemingly never ending barrage of puppy kisses, she was lovingly caressing the dog's butter-colored neck when her hand brushed against a small red silk bag that had been tied on with a red velvet ribbon. She'd almost missed it. Perplexed, wrinkles creased her suntanned brow as she asked "What's this?"

"What's what?" Ben responded guilelessly.

"This bag," she said, raising her head and eyeing him suspiciously.

Bending over and scrunching his face with mock confusion, he said, "Huh, that's really odd. I didn't notice it before. Maybe you better open it and see what's inside. Might be something important."

With shaking hands, Becca carefully untied the delicate bag off the excited pup. She pulled open the drawstring to find a tiny white box with the name of a family-owned jewelry store in Lake City. Instantly her heart began to flutter and she looked questioningly up at the tall man who suddenly knelt down in front of her and took the small box out of her hand. Opening the lid to reveal the beautiful square cut diamond engagement ring, he looked her straight in those emerald green eyes and said, "Rebecca Irene Thornton, I have loved you since before we even met. You've been a part of my dreams since I first understood there was a difference between boys and girls, but I never believed the girl of my dreams could be real. It was your strength of character and that wonderful – if sometimes sarcastic - sense of humor that attracted me to you immediately when your car broke down. That was certainly my lucky day! Of course, I couldn't begin to know how beautiful you are, but frankly, that didn't matter to me. I fell in love with your soul long before I was witness to your stunning Irish beauty. Now, I can't imagine living in a world without you beside me. Please say you'll marry me, Becca, and put me out of my misery?"

For the first time since the two had met all those months ago, Becca was speechless. Tears of happiness ran unchecked down her cheek and her throat closed up with emotion, so she simply nodded her head and hugged him tightly.

Cocking his head to one side, Ben quipped, "You do realize that you're going to have to actually answer out loud when the minister asks you "if you take this man," don't you?" as he slid the sparkling diamond on her finger.

Laughing out loud, Becca retorted, "I guess I'll have to work on that."

"Just so long as it doesn't take too long!" Ben responded as he picked her up once again and kissed away her tears while the pup barked excitedly and danced around the young couple.

EPILOGUE

The forest had come alive with the sounds and smells of spring. Squirrels chittered at each other as they jumped from tree to tree. Chipmunks chased each other among the brambles. A cacophony of birdsong filled the air and the roar of the snow melt filled brook as an open invitation to all forest creatures to come drink from its icy water. Lacey patterns of sunlight dappled the earth through the tree branches.

Near a large group of boulders at the edge of the meadow, a lone she-wolf licked her fur after finishing the cotton-tailed rabbit she had managed to catch this morning. The injury to her head she had sustained during the battle with the ranger had long since healed, but the one to her leg had never healed properly and slowed her mobility down considerably. That she had been able to capture the rabbit at all filled her with absolute delight. Since losing the rest of her pack during the attack on the ranger, she had been barely surviving by eating mostly bugs and the occasional unwary frog, but today she had managed to make her first significant kill. Being injured and on her own for the past few months had been difficult, but her survival instincts remained strong.

From her spot deeply hidden in the brush inside the tree line, she watched a young family walking along the water. Every once in a while, the little boy of five or so would run ahead to pick up some rock or pine cone he had discovered. Then his parents would call him back and they would delight in his found treasure. The female wolf was naturally wary of these trespassers and her eyes never left the trio until they had moved far beyond her sight. It wasn't that she was scared of these creatures, for she remembered facing one of their kind before, but she was wise enough to avoid any confrontation with them. For now, at least, her stomach was full and she was content to simply lay back and rest her aching body. She could feel the contractions beginning to build and knew that her time was very near. She had no memory of the notch-eared wolf that had sired her litter. She only knew that in the next few hours her pups would be whelped and before long a new pack would be running through the forest.

It was near dark and a sprinkling of stars had begun to come out by the time she rose from her place in the dirt. Moving her awkward body carefully to the stream, she dipped her russet-colored head down and drank her fill. Instinctively, she knew that once she began the birthing process in earnest, she wouldn't be leaving the pups to either eat or drink. That was another reason why the welcome gift of the rabbit was so fortunate. Her thirst quenched for the time being, she paused long enough to urinate before waddling back into the small den she had dug out from among the rocks over a month ago. Within the hollows gloom, the dame raked up the dried grass into a small mound. Lying on her side, she let out a deep sigh of contentment. Closing her eyes, she would doze lightly while waiting for the inevitable.

THE END

About the Author

Terry Hebert lives in Dallas, Texas with her husband of 43 years, Jack. She didn't begin writing books until her two children were grown and gone with children of their own. Always good for a tall tale, her family encouraged her to start writing down her literary ideas so others could enjoy them. So, she did. Winter of the Wolf is the first of her novels to be published.

Made in the
USA
Monee, IL